Penguin Books
Galahad at Blandings

Pelham Grenville Wodehouse was born in 1881 in Guildford, the son of a civil servant, and educated at Dulwich College. He spent a brief period working for the Hong Kong and Shanghai Bank before abandoning finance for writing, earning a living by journalism and selling stories to magazines.

An enormously popular and prolific writer, he produced about a hundred books, and was probably best known for creating Jeeves, the ever resourceful 'gentleman's personal gentleman', and the good-hearted young blunderer Bertie Wooster. However, Wodehouse created many other comic figures, perhaps most notably the inhabitants of, and regular visitors to, Blandings Castle and its environs. He wrote the many Blandings stories over the course of more than sixty years; the first, *Something Fresh*, appeared in 1915, while at the time of his death he was working on the posthumously published *Sunset at Blandings*. He was part-author and writer of fifteen straight plays and of 250 lyrics for some thirty musical comedies. *The Times* hailed him as a 'comic genius recognized in his lifetime as a classic and an old master of farce'.

P. G. Wodehouse said, 'I believe there are two ways of writing novels. One is mine, making a sort of musical comedy without music and ignoring real life altogether; the other is going right deep down into life and not caring a damn.'

Wodehouse married in 1914 and took American citizenship in 1955. He was created a Knight of the British Empire in the 1975 New Year's Honours List. In a BBC interview he said that he had no ambitions left now that he had been knighted and there was a waxwork of him in Madame Tussaud's. He died on St Valentine's Day, 1975, at the age of ninety-three.

P. G. Wodehouse in Penguin

P. G. Wodehouse
Galahad at Blandings

P.G.Wodehouse

Galahad
at
Blandings

PENGUIN BOOKS

PENGUIN BOOKS

Published by the Penguin Group
Penguin Books Ltd, 80 Strand, London WC2R 0RL, England
Penguin Putnam Inc., 375 Hudson Street, New York, New York 10014, USA
Penguin Books Australia Ltd, 250 Camberwell Road, Camberwell, Victoria 3124, Australia
Penguin Books Canada Ltd, 10 Alcorn Avenue, Toronto, Ontario, Canada M4V 3B2
Penguin Books India (P) Ltd, 11 Community Centre, Panchsheel Park, New Delhi – 110 017, India
Penguin Books (NZ) Ltd, Cnr Rosedale and Airborne Roads, Albany, Auckland, New Zealand
Penguin Books (South Africa) (Pty) Ltd, 24 Sturdee Avenue, Rosebank 2196, South Africa

Penguin Books Ltd, Registered Offices: 80 Strand, London WC2R 0RL, England

www.penguin.com

First published by Herbert Jenkins Ltd 1965
First published in Penguin Books 1966
5

Set in 9/11pt Monotype Trump
Typeset by Rowland Phototypesetting Ltd,
Bury St Edmunds, Suffolk
Printed in England by Clays Ltd, St Ives plc

1

Of the two young men sharing a cell in one of New York's popular police stations Tipton Plimsoll, the tall thin one, was the first to recover, if only gradually, from the effect of the potations which had led to his sojourn in the coop. The other, Wilfred Allsop, pint-size and fragile and rather like the poet Shelley in appearance, was still asleep.

For some time after life had returned to the rigid limbs Tipton sat with his head between his hands, the better to prevent it floating away from the parent neck. He was still far from feeling at the peak of his form and would have given much for a cake of ice against which to rest his forehead, but he was deriving a certain solace from the thought that his betrothed, Veronica, only daughter of Colonel and Lady Hermione Wedge of Rutland Gate, London SW7, was three thousand miles away and would never learn of his doings this summer night. He was also reviewing the past, trying to piece together the events that had led up to the tragedy, and little by little they began to come back to him.

The party in the Greenwich Village studio. Quite a good party, with sculptors, *avant garde* playwrights and other local fauna dotted around, busy with their bohemian revels. There had occurred that morning on the New York Stock Exchange one of those slumps or crashes which periodically spoil the day for Stock Exchanges, but it had not touched the lives of residents in the Washington Square neighbourhood, where intellect reigns and little interest is taken in the fluctuations of the money market. Unmoved by the news in the evening papers that Amalgamated Cheese had closed twenty points off and Consolidated Hamburgers fifteen, the members of the party, most of whom would not have known a stock certificate from a greeting card, were all cutting up and having a good time, and so was Tipton. The large fortune he had recently inherited from a deceased uncle was invested in the shares of Tipton's Stores, which never varied more than a point or two, no matter what financial earthquakes might be happening elsewhere.

Over in a corner of this Greenwich Village studio he had perceived a pint-size character at the piano, tickling the ivories with a skill that commanded admiration. His compliments to this pint-size bozo on his virtuosity. The 'Oh, thanks awfully' which betrayed the other's English origin. The subsequent fraternization. The exchange of names. The quick start of surprise on the bozo's part. Plimsoll, did you say? Not *Tipton* Plimsoll? Sure. Are you the chap who's engaged to Veronica Wedge? That's right. Do you know her? She's my cousin. She's what? My cousin. You mean you're Vee's *cousin*? Have been for years. Well, fry me for an oyster, I think this calls for a drink, don't you?

And that was how it had all begun. Circumstances, it came out in the course of conversation, had rendered Wilfred Allsop low-spirited, and when he sees a friend low-spirited, especially a friend linked by ties of blood to the girl he loves, the man of sensibility spares no effort or expense to alleviate his depression and bring the roses back to his cheeks. One beaker had led to another, the lessons learned at mother's knee had been temporarily forgotten, and here they were, behind bars.

Tipton had been nursing his throbbing head for perhaps a quarter of an hour and had just assured himself by delicate experiment that it was not, as he had at one time feared, going to explode like a high-powered shell, when a soft moan in his rear caused him to turn. Wilfred Allsop was sitting up, his face pale, his eyes glassy, his hair disordered. He looked like the poet Shelley after a big night out with Lord Byron.

'What's this place?' he asked in a faint whisper. 'Is it a jug of some description?'

'That's just about what it is, Willie. We call them hoosegows over here, but the general effect is the same. How's the boy?'

'What boy?'

'You.'

'Oh, me? I'm dying.'

'Of course you're not.'

'Yes, I am,' said Wilfred with some asperity. A man is entitled to know whether he is dying or not. 'And before I pass on there's something I want you to promise you'll do for me. If you're engaged to Vee, I take it you've visited Blandings Castle?'

'Sure. It was there I met her.'

'Well, did you happen, while there, to run into a girl called Monica Simmons?'

'The name doesn't ring a bell. Who is she?'

'She looks after Empress of Blandings, that pig of my Uncle Clarence's.'

'Ah, then I've seen her. Old Emsworth took me to the sty a couple of times and she was there, ladling out the bran mash. Girl who looks like an all-in wrestler.'

Wilfred's asperity became more marked. Their evening together had filled him with a deep affection for Tipton Plimsoll, but even from a great friend he could not countenance loose talk of this sort.

'I am sorry you think she looks like an all-in wrestler,' he said stiffly. 'To me she seems to resemble one of those Norse goddesses. However, be that as it may, I love her, Tippy. I fell in love with her at first sight.'

Recalling the picture of Miss Simmons in smock and trousers with a good deal of mud on her face, Tipton found this difficult to believe, but he was sympathetic.

'Good for you. Peach of a girl, I should imagine. Did you tell her so?'

'I couldn't do it. I hadn't the nerve. She's so majestic, and I'm such a little squirt. You agree that I'm a little squirt, Tippy?'

'Well, I don't know I'd put it just that way, but I guess one's got to face it, there are taller guys around.'

'All I've done so far is look at her and talk about the weather.'

'Not much percentage in that.'

'No, the whole thing's quite hopeless. But here's what I was starting to say. I want you, when I am gone, to see that she gets my cigarette case. It's all I have to leave. Can I trust you to do this when I have passed beyond the veil?'

'You aren't going to pass beyond the veil.'

'I *am* going to pass beyond the veil,' said Wilfred petulantly. 'You've made a note of what I was saying. Cigarette case. To be given to Monica Simmons after my decease.'

'Does she smoke?'

'Of course she smokes.'

'She'll be able to blow smoke rings at the pig.'

Wilfred stiffened.

'There is no need to be flippant about it, Plimsoll. I am asking you as a friend to perform this small act of kindness for me. Can I rely on you?'

'Sure. I'll attend to it.'

'Tell her my last thoughts were of her and I expired with her name on my lips.'

'Okay.'

'Thank you, thank you, thank you,' said Wilfred, and went to sleep again.

2

Deprived of human companionship, Tipton felt sad and lonely. He was a gregarious soul and it always made him uneasy when he had no one to talk to. Throughout these exchanges with Wilfred Allsop he had been aware of a policeman pacing up and down the corridor on the other side of the bars, and policemen, while often not ideal as conversationalists, being inclined to confine themselves to monosyllables and those spoken out of the side of their mouths, are better than nothing. He went to the bars and peering through them like some rare specimen in a zoo, uttered a husky 'Hey, officer.'

The policeman was a long, stringy policeman, who flowed out of his uniform at odd spots. His face was gnarled, his wrists knobbly and of a geranium hue, and he had those three or four extra inches of neck which disqualify a man for high honours in a beauty competition. But beneath this forbidding exterior there lay a kindly heart and he could make allowances for the indiscretions of youth. Muggers, stick-up men and hoodlums in general he disliked, but towards the Tipton type of malefactor he was able to be indulgent. So where to one of his ordinary clientele he would have replied with a brusque 'Pipe down, youse,' he now said 'Hi' in a not uncordial voice and joined Tipton at the bars, through which they proceeded to converse like a modern Pyramus and Thisbe.

'How's it coming?' he asked.

Tipton replied that he had a headache, and the policeman said that that occasioned him no surprise.

'You certainly earned it, Mac.'

'I guess I was kind of high.'

'You sure were,' said the policeman. 'The boys were saying it took three of them to get you into the paddy wagon.'

His manner had not been censorious and his voice

had contained admiration rather than reproof, but
nevertheless Tipton felt it incumbent on him to justify
himself.

'You mustn't think I do this sort of thing often,' he
said. 'At one time, yes, but not since I became engaged. I
promised my fiancée I'd go easy on the nights of wine
and roses. But this was a special case. I was trying to
cheer up my friend over there and bring a little sunshine
into his life.'

'Feeling low, was he?'

'In the depths, officer, and with reason. He was telling
me the whole story. He's a musician. Plays the piano
and composes things. He came here from England some
months ago hoping to crash Tin Pan Alley or get taken
on by one of the bands, but couldn't make the grade.
Ran out of money and had to cable home for supplies.'

'And the folks wouldn't send him none?'

'Oh sure, they sent him enough to buy his passage to
England. He leaves the day after tomorrow. But his Aunt
Hermione said it was high time he stopped fooling
around and settled down to a regular job, and she'd
found one for him. And do you know what that job is?
Teaching music in a girls' school. And that's not all. The
woman who runs the school is a rabid Dry and won't let
her staff so much as look at a snifter. It means that poor
old Willie won't be able to take aboard the simplest
highball except in vacation time.'

'What he had tonight ought to last him quite a while.'

'Don't mock, officer, don't scoff,' said Tipton,
frowning. 'The thing's a tragedy. It has absolutely
shattered Willie, and I don't wonder. There was a guy at
the Drones Club in London, of which I am a member,
who once got roped in to make a speech to a girls'
school, and he never really recovered from the
experience. To this day he trembles like a leaf if he sees
anything in a straw hat and a blazer, with pigtails down
its back. Teaching a bunch of girls music will be ten

times worse. They'll put their heads together and whisper. They'll nudge each other and giggle. They'll probably throw spitballs at him. And nothing to strengthen him for the ordeal but lemonade and sarsaparilla. But I notice you're yawning. I'm not keeping you up, am I?'

The policeman said he was not. He was, he explained, on all night duty and was glad of a chat to while the time away.

'Fine,' said Tipton, reassured. 'Yes, I can imagine you must find it pretty dull without anyone to shoot the breeze with. It can't be all jam being a cop.'

'You can say that again.'

'Still, you have compensations.'

'Name three.'

'Well, you meet such interesting people – bandits, porch climbers, dope pushers, sex fiends and what not. The whole boiling from deadbeats to millionaires.'

'We don't get a lot of millionaires.'

'You don't?'

'Never seen one myself.'

'Is that so? Well, you're seeing one now. Take a gander.'

The policeman stared.

'You?'

'Me.'

'No kidding?'

'None whatever. You know Tipton's Stores?'

'Sure. The wife does her marketing there.'

'Well, tell her when you get home that you were host tonight to the guy who owns the controlling interest in them. My Uncle Chet founded Tipton's Stores. He checked out not long ago and I inherited his block of shares, practically all there are. I'm rolling.'

'Then why don't you pay your ten bucks and get out of here?'

'What ten bucks?'

'For bail. I'd do it if it was me.'

A bitter laugh escaped Tipton, the sort of laugh a toad beneath the harrow might have uttered if some passer-by had asked it why it did not move from beneath the harrow, where conditions must be far from comfortable.

'I dare say you would,' he said, 'and so would I if I had the dough. But I've no funds of any description. Oh, I don't mean I've been wiped out in this Stock Exchange crash they've been having – I may be a chump, but I'm not chump enough to play the market – but I don't have a nickel on me at the moment. At some point in this evening's proceedings some child of unmarried parents got away with my entire wad, leaving me without a cent. I own a controlling interest in the country's largest supermarket, with branches in every town in the United States. I own a ranch out west. I own an apartment house on Park Avenue. I even own a music publishing business in London. But I can't get out of this darned dungeon because I haven't ten dollars in my kick. Can you beat that for irony?'

The policeman said he was unable to, but seemed to see no cause for despair.

'You got friends, ain't you?'

'Lashings of them.'

'Well, why don't you phone one of them and get him to help you out?'

Tipton was surprised.

'Do they let you phone from here?'

'You're allowed one call.'

'Is that the law?'

'That's the law.'

'Then . . . Oh, finished your little nap, Willie?'

Wilfred Allsop had risen, blinked his eyes several times, groaned, shuddered from head to foot and was now joining the party. He seemed in slightly better shape than on the occasion of his previous resurrection. His resemblance to a corpse that had been in the water several days was still pronounced, but it had become a cheerier corpse, one that had begun to look on the bright side.

'Oh, Tippy,' he said, 'I thought you would be interested to know that I'm not going to die. I'm feeling a little better.'

'That's the spirit.'

'Not much better, but a little. So never mind about the cigarette case. Who's that you're talking to? I can't see him very distinctly, but isn't he a policeman?'

'That's right.'

'Do you think he could tell us how to get out of here?'

'The very point I was discussing with him when you came to the surface. He says the hellhounds of the system will release us if we slip them ten bucks apiece.'

Wilfred's mind was still clouded, but he was capable of formulating an idea.

'Let's slip them ten bucks apiece,' he suggested.

'How? You haven't any dough, have you?'

'None.'

'Nor have I. Somebody swiped my roll. But this gentleman, Mr – ?'

'Garroway.'

'Mr Garroway here says I can phone a friend for some.'

Again Wilfred Allsop had a constructive proposal to put forward.

'Go and phone a friend for some.'

Tipton shook his head, and uttered a sharp howl. There are times when shaking the head creates the illusion that one has met Jael the wife of Heber, incurred her displeasure and started her going into her celebrated routine.

'It isn't as simple as all that. There's a catch. One's only allowed one call.'

'I don't get your point.'

'Then you must be still stewed. You get it, don't you, Mr Garroway?'

'Sure. Your buddy mightn't be there. Then you'll have used up your call and got nowheres.'

'Exactly. It's the middle of August and all the guys I know are out of town. They'll be coming back after Labour Day, but it won't be Labour Day for another three weeks, and we don't want to have to wait till then. Gosh, I wish you wouldn't do that,' said Tipton, wincing.

He was alluding to a sudden sharp barking sound which had proceeded from his fellow prisoner's lips. It had affected his head unpleasantly, creating the passing impression that someone had touched off a stick or two of dynamite inside it.

'Sorry,' said Wilfred. 'I was thinking of Uncle Clarence.'

The statement did nothing to mollify Tipton. He said with a good deal of bitterness that that did credit to a nephew's heart. It was nice of him, he said, to think of his Uncle Clarence.

'He's in New York. He's at the Plaza. He came over here for my Aunt Constance's wedding. She was marrying a Yank called Schoonmaker.'

Tipton saw that he had judged his friend too hastily. What he had taken for an idle changing of the subject had been in reality most pertinent to the issue.

'That's right,' he exclaimed. 'I read about it in the papers. This begins to look good. You're sure he's at the Plaza?'

'Certain. Aunt Hermione told me to go and look him up there.'

'But can I wake him at this time of night?'

'If you explain that it's an emergency. You'll have to make it quite clear that your need is urgent. You know what a muddle headed old ass he is.'

This was perfectly true. Clarence, ninth Earl of Emsworth, that vague and dreamy peer, was not one of England's keenest brains. The life he led made for slowness of the thinking processes. Except when he was attending sisters' weddings in America, he spent his time pottering about the gardens and messuages of Blandings Castle, his rural seat, his thoughts, such as they were, concentrated on his prize sow, Empress of Blandings. When indoors you could generally find him in his study engrossed in a book of porcine interest, most frequently that monumental work *On The Care Of The Pig* by Augustus Whipple (Popgood and Grooly, thirty-five shillings), of which he never wearied.

Tipton's first enthusiasm had begun to wane. Like Hamlet, he had become irresolute. He chewed his lower lip dubiously.

'It's taking a big chance. Suppose he's out on a toot somewhere?'

'Is it likely that a staid old bird like Uncle Clarence would go on toots?'

'You never know.'

'If it was my Uncle Galahad, I wouldn't say, but surely not Uncle Clarence.'

'It's a possibility that has to be taken into consideration. The most respectable of Limeys get it up their noses and start stepping out when they come to New York. It's the air here. Very heady. What would you do in a case like this, Mr Garroway?'

The policeman fingered a chin modelled on the ram of a battleship. There was a rasping sound as he scratched it.

'Lemme get it straight. You want to make sure the guy's in?'

'The whole enterprise depends on that.'

'Well, how about me calling him first? If he answers, it'll mean he's there and I'll hang up. Then you give him a buzz.'

Tipton eyed him reverently. A Daniel come to judgement, he was feeling. If this was the normal level of intelligence in New York's police force, it was not to be wondered at that they were known as The Finest.

'God bless you, Garroway,' he said emotionally,
'you've solved the whole problem. Tell Mrs Garroway
next time she shops at Tipton's Stores to mention my
name and say I said she was to have anything she wants
on the house, from certified butter to prime rib of beef
and chicken noodle soup.'

'Very kind of you, sir. She'll be tickled pink. The Plaza
I think you said, and your buddy's name is Clarence?'

'Emsworth.'

'My mistake.'

'Ask for the Earl of Emsworth. He's a lord.'

'Oh, one of those? Right.'

3

The officer hurried off, and Tipton gazed after him,
awed.

'What malarkey people talk about the New York
police being brutal,' he said. 'Brutal, my left eyeball. I
never met a sweeter guy, did you?'

'Never.'

'You can hear the milk of human kindness sloshing
about inside him.'

'Distinctly.'

'It wouldn't surprise me to find he'd started life as a
Boy Scout.'

'Nor me.'

'It shows how silly it is to go by people's looks. It's
not his fault that he's no oil painting.'

'Of course not.'

'And what is beauty, after all?'

'Exactly. Skin deep, I often say.'

'So do I, frequently.'

'It's the heart that counts.'

'Every time. And his is as big as the Yankee Stadium.
Ah, Garroway. What's the score?'

'He's there.'

'Three – no, make it four – rousing cheers. How did he seem?'

'Sleepy.'

'I mean in what sort of mood? Amiable? Docile? Friendly? A likely prospect for the touch, did you feel?'

'Sure.'

'Then stand out of my way and let me get at that telephone,' said Tipton.

As he went, his head was still aching, but his heart was light. He was about to embark on a course of action which would fill the bosoms of several of his fellow creatures, notably Colonel and Lady Hermione Wedge, with alarm and despondency, but he did not know this. He was not clairvoyant.

2

1

The Blandings Castle of which mention was made in the
previous chapter of this chronicle stands on a knoll of
rising ground at the southern end of the Vale of
Blandings in the county of Shropshire. It came into
existence towards the middle of the fifteenth century at
a time when the landed gentry of England, who never
knew when a besieging army might not be coming
along, particularly if they lived close to the Welsh
border, believed in building their little nests solid. Huge
and grey and majestic, adorned with turrets and
battlements in great profusion, it unquestionably takes
the eye. Even Tipton Plimsoll, though not as a rule given
to poetic rhapsodies, had become lyrical on first
beholding it, making a noise with his tongue like the
popping of a cork and saying 'Some joint!' The
illustrated weeklies often print articles about it
accompanied by photographs showing the park, the
gardens, the yew alley and its other attractions. In these
its proprietor, Clarence, ninth Earl of Emsworth,
sometimes appears, looking like an absent-minded
member of the Jukes family, for he has always been a
careless dresser and when in front of a camera is inclined
to let his mouth hang open in rather a noticeable way.

On a fine morning a few days after the hand of the
law had fallen on Tipton and his fiancée's cousin Wilfred
Allsop the beauty of the noble building was enhanced by
the presence outside it of Sebastian Beach, the castle
butler. He was standing beside a luggage-laden car which

was drawn up at the front door, waiting to give an official send-off to Lord Emsworth's younger brother Galahad, who, with his niece Veronica Wedge, was about to drive to London to pick up the ninth Earl on his return from America.

As is so often the case with butlers, there was a good deal of Beach. Julius Caesar, who liked to have men about him that were fat, would have taken to him at once. He was a man who had made two chins grow where only one had been before, and his waistcoat swelled like the sail of a racing yacht. You would never have thought, to look at him, that forty years ago he had come in first in a choir boys' bicycle race, open to those whose voices had not broken by the first Sunday in Epiphany, and that only two days before the start of this story he had won the Market Blandings Darts Tournament, outshooting such seasoned experts as Jno. Robinson, who ran the station taxi cab, and Percy Bulstrode, the local chemist.

He had been standing there for some minutes, when a brisk, dapper little gentleman in the early fifties appeared in the doorway and came down the steps. This was the Hon. Galahad Threepwood, a man disapproved of by his numerous sisters but considered in the Servants' Hall to shed lustre on Blandings Castle.

Gally Threepwood was the only genuinely distinguished member of the family of which Lord Emsworth was the head. Lord Emsworth himself had once won a first prize for pumpkins at the Shropshire Agricultural Show and his pig, Empress of Blandings, had three times been awarded the silver medal for fatness at that annual festival, but you could not say that he had really risen to eminence in the public life of England. Gally, on the other hand, had made a name for himself. The passage of the years had put him more or less in retirement now, but in his youth he had been one

of the lights of London, one of the great figures at whom
the world of the stage, the racecourse and the rowdier
restaurants had pointed with pride. There were men in
London – bookmakers, skittle sharps, jellied eel sellers
at race meetings and the like – who would have been
puzzled to know whom you were referring to if you had
spoken of Einstein, but they were all familiar with
Gally.

He was soberly dressed now for his visit to London,
but even in this decorous costume he seemed to bring
with him a whiff of the paddock and the American bar.
He still gave the impression that he was wearing a
checked coat, tight trousers and a grey bowler hat and
that there were race glasses bumping against his left hip.
His bright eyes, one of them adorned with a
black-rimmed monocle, seemed to be watching horses
rounding into the straight, his neatly shod foot to be
pawing in search of a brass rail.

He greeted Beach with the easy cordiality of a friend
of long standing. There had existed between them a
perfect *rapport* since they had both been slips of boys of
forty. Each respected and admired the other for his many
gifts.

'Hullo, Beach. Lovely morning.'

'Yes, sir.'

Gally looked at him sharply. The sombreness of his
voice had surprised him. Scanning his face, he could see
that it was a dull purple colour and that the lower of his
two chins was quivering.

'Something the matter, Beach? You have the air of a
man whose soul is not at rest. What's wrong?'

From anyone else the butler would have hidden his
secret sorrow, but everybody confided in Gally.
Barmaids poured out their troubles to him, and the
humblest racecourse tout knew that he could rely on
him for sympathy and understanding.

'I have been grossly insulted, Mr Galahad.'

'You have? Who by? Or by whom, as the case may be?'

'The young gentleman.'

'You don't mean Wilfred Allsop?'

'No, sir. Master Winkworth.'

'Oh, Huxley? Unpleasant brat, that. And yet his mother dotes on him, which just shows there's no accounting for tastes. What did he say?'

'He criticized my personal appearance.'

'He must be hard to please.'

'Yes, sir,' said Beach, prepared now to withhold nothing. He had been wanting a friendly shoulder to cry on ever since the affront to his dignity had occurred. 'He told me that I was fatter than Empress of Blandings.'

No vestige of a smile appeared on Gally's face. He was all kindly reassurance.

'You mustn't pay any attention to what a little wart like that says. He only does it to annoy, because he knows it teases. I hope you treated him with the contempt he deserved.'

'I'm afraid I came within an ace of clipping him on the side of the head, Mr Galahad.'

'It would have done him all the good in the world, but I'm glad you didn't. It wouldn't have pleased his mother. But don't let his critique worry you. Admittedly you get your money's worth out of a weighing machine and if your body were fished out of the Thames it would be described as that of a well-nourished man of middle age, but what of it? I rather envy you. I could do with a few more pounds myself. Odd,' said Gally thoughtfully, 'how sensitive people are about their weight. I am reminded of Chet Tipton. Did I ever tell you about Chet Tipton?'

'Not to my recollection, Mr Galahad.'

'Uncle of the chap who's marrying my niece Veronica. American, but spent a good deal of his time over here and I used to see a lot of him at the old Pelican Club. Enormously fat fellow. People used to chaff him about it, so at last he decided to buy one of those abdominal belts you see advertised. Rubber they're made of and you clamp them round your tummy and melt inside them. Well, naturally they have to be a pretty tight fit and Chet could hardly breathe in his and of course could take no solid nourishment, but he stuck to it because he knew how slim it was making him look, and he was having a buttered rum in the Criterion bar one morning instead of lunch, when a friend of his came in and said "Hullo, Chet", and he said "Hullo, George or Jack or Jimmy or whatever the name was", and they chatted for a while, and then the chap said "Aren't you rather stouter than when I saw you last? I'll tell you what you ought to do, Chet. You ought to get one of those abdominal belts". He gave it up after that. Sort of discouraged him. Dead now, poor fellow, as so many of the old crowd are. Yes, only a few of us left now. Well, is the luggage all in?'

'Yes, sir.'

'Then if I'm going to pick Clarence up for lunch, we ought to be starting. What's the time?'

Beach drew from the pocket of his spreading waistcoat the handsome silver watch bestowed on him as the prize in the Market Blandings Darts Tournament. It was his dearest possession and never failed to give him a thrill when he looked at it.

'Just on ten, Mr Galahad.'

'Well, dash in and tell that Wedge girl to get a move on. Ah, here she is. No, it's only Sandy Callender.'

2

The girl who was coming down the steps was in many respects a most agreeable sight for the eye to rest on. Her figure was trim, her nose and mouth above criticism and her hair that attractive red that Titian used to admire so much. But to a connoisseur of beauty like Gally the whole effect was spoiled by the tortoiseshell-rimmed spectacles she was wearing. They seemed to cover most of her face, and he wondered when she had taken to them. There had been no sign of them at their last meeting, though of course she may have had them tucked away in her bag.

'Hullo, young Sandy,' he said.

Alexandra ('Sandy') Callender and he were old friends. She had been working for the late Chet Tipton when he had first known her, and it was he who had obtained for her the post of secretary to his brother Clarence, a fact which he hoped would never come to his brother Clarence's knowledge, for his reproaches would have been hard to bear. Lord Emsworth was, and always had been, allergic to secretaries.

'You look very dusty, Sandy. Have you been rolling in something?'

'I've been cleaning out Lord Emsworth's study.'

'Poor devil.'

'Me?'

'Clarence. He hates having his study cleaned.'

'Does he like a mess?'

'He loves it. It's his idea of comfort. Well, you seem to have been putting in some strenuous work. Your appearance brings to mind a headline I saw in a paper once about Sons Of Toil Buried Beneath Tons Of Soil. Still, if it makes you happy.'

'Oh, I'm quite happy. Gally, I wonder if you would mind posting this parcel in London for me.'

'Of course.'

'Thank you,' said Sandy, and went back into the house.

Gally looked after her thoughtfully. There had been a certain something in her manner that gave him the impression that she was not as happy as she had stated herself to be, and it disturbed him. It was not the first time he had noticed this. She had been below par since her arrival. In the Chet Tipton days he had found her a merry little soul, always good for a couple of laughs, but Blandings Castle seemed to have depressed her. Brooding on something, unless he was very much mistaken. He scanned the parcel, noting the address.

'S. G. Bagshott, 4 Halsey Chambers, Halsey Court, London W1. Unusual name. There can't be many Bagshotts around. I wonder if he's any relation to my old friend Boko. You remember Boko Bagshott, Beach?'

'I fear not, Mr Galahad. I do not think he was ever a visitor at the castle.'

'That's right, I don't believe he ever was. I used to see him in London and at a whacking big house he had down in Sussex near Petworth. Interesting personality. He made a practice every year of kidding some insurance company that he wanted to insure his life for a hundred thousand pounds or so and after the doctors had examined him telling them he had changed his mind. He thus got an annual medical check-up for nothing.'

'Ingenious, Mr Galahad.'

'Very. One of the brightest brains in the old Pelican. This chap might quite easily be his son. He had a son called Samuel Galahad. I recall that distinctly. He named him Samuel after Sam Bowles the jockey and Galahad because he was a bit superstitious and thought it might lead to the boy inheriting what he supposed to be my ability to spot winners. Not that I ever did spot many winners, but he always had a great respect for my judgement after I gave him a hundred to eight shot for the Jubilee Cup. He used to come to me before every important meeting and seek my advice. I wonder what young Sandy is sending him parcels about. There is a squashiness about this one that excites the interest. It feels as if –'

He would have spoken further of the parcel's squashiness and its possible contents, but at this moment an interruption occurred. A vision of beauty had appeared at the head of the steps, a girl of a radiant blonde loveliness that would have drawn a whistle from the least susceptible of the Armed Forces of the United States of America. Nature had not given Veronica Wedge more than about as much brain as would fit comfortably into an aspirin bottle, feeling no doubt that it was better not to overdo the thing, but apart from that she had everything and it is scarcely surprising that Tipton Plimsoll, when he spoke of her, did so with a catch in his throat and a tremolo in his voice.

She was followed by her mother, Lord Emsworth's sister Hermione, at whom not even Don Juan or Casanova would have whistled. Lady Hermione Wedge was the only one of the female members of the Emsworth family who was not statuesquely handsome. She was short and dumpy and looked like a cook – in her softer moods a cook well satisfied with her latest soufflé; when stirred to anger a cook about to give notice; but always a cook of strong character. Her husband, Colonel Egbert Wedge, was as wax in her hands, as was her daughter Veronica.

The parcel attracted her attention.

'What have you got there, Galahad?'

'It's something squashy the Callender girl wants me to post for her in London. Amazing that she has time to pack parcels with all the charlady work she's doing in Clarence's study. She's certainly a competent secretary. Poor old Clarence!'

'What do you mean, poor old Clarence?'

'Well, you know how he dislikes competent secretaries. They bother him and get on his nerves. They keep him from evading his responsibilities.'

'What does evading his responsibilities mean, Mummee?' said Veronica.

It was the sort of question she frequently asked, and as a rule her mother was prompt with patient explanations, sometimes taking as much as ten minutes over them, but now she found herself ignored. Lady Hermione's thoughts were not on her offspring. Gally's monocle had just flashed in the morning sun and she was thinking how much she disliked it. In common with all her sisters she considered Gally a disgrace to a proud family and a blot on the escutcheon, but she sometimes felt that she could have borne him with more fortitude if he had not worn a monocle. There were book-makers and racecourse touts who held a similar view. Widely differing from Lady Hermione on almost every other point, they became, as she did, uncomfortable beneath the glare of Gally's black-rimmed eye-glass.

'Clarence must be made to realize that he cannot evade his responsibilities. The one thing he needs is a good secretary. Left to himself, he would never answer his letters.'

His letters! A blinding light flashed upon Gally.

'Excuse me a moment,' he said, and leaped lissomely up the steps and into the house. Lady Hermione looked after him frowningly, her lips set. She liked him least when he behaved like a pea on a hot shovel.

3

Sandy was in Lord Emsworth's study, more than ever encrusted with dust and deep in documents which should have been attended to weeks before. She looked up, surprised, as Gally came trotting in.

'Haven't you gone yet?'

'The start of the expedition has been postponed in order that I may have a word with you. Busy?'

'Very.'

'Wait till Clarence sees your handiwork. He'll have a fit. For God's sake don't ever let him know that it was I who got you the job. Well, young Sandy, so you're sending the boy friend back his letters, are you?'

She started, dislodging a bill for goods supplied which had managed to get entangled in her hair.

'I don't know what you mean!'

'No good trying to fool me, child. I know what's in this parcel. Correct me if I'm wrong, but this is the set-up as I see it. You were engaged to this S. G. Bagshott. For a time you thought him the only onion in the stew. Then you had a fight about something and relations deteriorated to the point where you told him those wedding bells would not ring out. Take back your ring, you said, take back the bottle of scent you gave me on my birthday, you said, and now you're returning his letters. Am I right?'

'More or less.'

'And you really want me to post this parcel?'

'Yes.'

'This is the end, is it?'

'Yes.'

'What did the poor fish do to make you mad? How do you know the girl you saw him kissing wasn't his aunt?'

'I did not see him kissing a girl.'

'Well, what put you off him? Did he step on your foot while dancing? Did he criticize your hair-do? Lose your umbrella? Take you out of a business double?'

'If you don't mind, Gally, I've a lot of work to do.'

'What you mean is, Don't be such a damned old Nosey Parker. All right, if you insist. But I'm going to find out what the trouble was. What does that S of his stand for?'

'Samuel.'

'I thought as much. It now becomes pretty certain that he's the son of an old friend of mine and has a claim on my interest. I shall call on him and deliver this parcel in person. He'll give me the facts, and the betting is that I shall bring you two young sundered hearts together again. Sundered hearts make me sick,' said Gally. 'I've been against them from boyhood.'

3

Halsey Court, though situated in Mayfair and entitled to
put 'London W.1.' after its name, is not a fashionable
locality. It is a small, dark, dingy cul-de-sac, far too full
of prowling cats, fluttering newspapers and derelict
banana skins to attract the *haut monde*. Dukes avoid it,
marquises give it a wide berth, earls and viscounts
would not settle there if you paid them. It consists of
some seedy offices and a block of residential flats,
Halsey Chambers, which are occupied mostly by young
men of slender means who cannot afford to pick and
choose and are thankful to have an inexpensive roof
over their heads. Jeff Miller, the writer of novels of
suspense, lived there at one time; so did Jerry Shoesmith,
editor until his services were dispensed with of the
weekly paper *Society Spice*; and now that they had
married and gone elsewhere literature was represented by
Sandy Callender's late betrothed, Samuel Galahad
Bagshott.

Actually, when he had forms to fill up and
information to give to an inquisitive bureaucracy, Sam
described himself as a barrister, but it was his typewriter
that enabled him to pay the rent and enjoy three
moderately square meals a day. Like so many
commencing barristers, he wrote assiduously while
waiting for the briefs to start coming in. He wrote short,
bright articles on fly fishing, healthy living, muscle
development, great lovers through the ages and the
modern girl. He wrote light verse, reviews of novels,

interviews with celebrities, chatty Guides to the Brontë country and the Land of Dickens, stories for halfwitted adults, stories for retarded boys and stories for children with water on the brain. It was with the last-named section of his public in mind that he was toiling on the morning when Gally had started his drive to London. He was writing a short story about a kitten called Pinky-Poo which he hoped, if all went well and the editor's heart was in the right place, to sell to the Yuletide number of *Wee Tots*.

He did not look the sort of young man from whom one would have expected stories about kittens called Pinky-Poo or indeed about kittens whose godparents had been less fanciful in their choice of names, for his appearance was distinctly on the rugged side. Tough was the adjective a stylist like Gustave Flaubert would have applied to him, though being French he would have said *dur* or *coriace*. He was large and chunky, he had been one of the Possibles in an England international Rugby trial game, and a fondness for boxing had left his nose a little out of the straight and one of his ears twisted. If he had been your guide to the Brontë country or the Land of Dickens, you would probably have felt a qualm at the thought of being alone with him on a deserted moor or down a dark alley, but your apprehensions would have been needless, for despite his intimidating looks he was inwardly, like Tipton Plimsoll's Officer Garroway, all sweetness and light. Off the football field and outside the ring anything in the shape of mayhem would have been unthinkable to him.

He had written the words 'There never was a naughtier kitten than Pinky-Poo' and was leaning back in his chair with the feeling that he was off to a good start but wondering what twists and turns his narrative would now take, when the doorbell rang. Going to answer it, he found standing on the mat a small, dapper,

elderly gentleman with an eye-glass who bade him a
civil good morning.

'Good morning,' said Sam, not to be outdone in the
courtesies. The thought occurred to him that this might
be a solicitor bringing a brief, but he did not really hope.
Solicitors, if they call on barristers, do so at their
chambers in Lincoln's Inn or wherever it may be, and
they seldom wear monocles and never beam as this
visitor was doing. Nor are they as a rule so rosy and
robust.

That was what struck Sam immediately about
Galahad Threepwood, that he looked extraordinarily fit
for his years. It was the impression Gally made on
everyone who met him. After the life he had led he had
no right to burst with health, but he did. Where most of
his contemporaries had long ago thrown in the towel
and retired to cure resorts to nurse their gout, he had
gone blithely on, ever rising on stepping stones of dead
whiskies and sodas to higher things. He had discovered
the prime grand secret of eternal youth – to keep the
decanter circulating, to stop smoking only when
snapping the lighter for his next cigarette and never to
retire to rest before three in the morning.

'Doesn't he look marvellous?' one of his nieces had
once said of him. 'It really is extraordinary that anyone
who has had as good a time as he has can be so
amazingly healthy. Everywhere you look you see men
leading model lives and pegging out in their prime, but
good old Uncle Gally, who apparently never went to
bed till he was fifty, is still breezing along as perky as
ever.'

'Yes?' said Sam.

'Mr Bagshott?'

'Yes.'

'My name is Threepwood.'

'Oh yes?'

'Galahad Threepwood.'

   The name touched a chord in Sam's memory. It was
one the late Berkeley Bagshott had often mentioned
when in reminiscent vein. The conversation of his
intimates of the old days was always inclined to turn to
Gally as they probed the past.

   'Oh, really?' he said, beaming in his turn. 'I've heard
my father speak of you.'

   'So you *are* old Boko's son? I thought so.'

   'You were great friends, weren't you?'

   'Bosom.'

   'That was why he had me christened Galahad, I
suppose.'

   'Yes, it was a pretty thought. He told me he would
have asked me to be your godfather, only he didn't feel it
would be safe. Starting you off under too much of a
handicap.'

   'Well, it's awfully nice of you to look me up. How did
you find my address?'

   'It was given me by Sandy Callender as I was leaving
Blandings Castle this morning.'

   'Oh?' Sam gulped. 'So you've met Sandy?'

   'I've known her for quite a time. We first met in New
York when she was working for Chet Tipton, a pal of
mine. He, poor chap, handed in his dinner pail and she
came to London, looking for a job. I ran into her just
when my sister Hermione was wanting a secretary for
my brother Clarence, so I recommended her and she was
signed on. This morning, as I was leaving, she gave me
this parcel to post. I saw your name, the S. G. struck me
as significant and I decided to deliver it in person, just in
case you were the fellow I thought you might be, if you
see what I mean. I don't know what odds a bookie would
have given me against your turning out to be Boko's son,
but it seemed a fair speculative venture, and the long
shot came off.'

   'I see. Er – how is Sandy?'

   'Physically fizzing, spiritually not so good. She has the

air of one who is brooding on something, as it might be a broken engagement or something of that kind. Am I right in supposing that this parcel contains your letters?'

Sam nodded gloomily.

'I expect so. She told me she was going to send them back.'

There was a world of sympathy in the eye behind Gally's monocle. As many people did, he had taken an instant liking to this son of one with whom he had so often heard the chimes of midnight, and he longed to do something to lighten his gloom. Years of membership of the old Pelican Club, where somebody was always having trouble with duns or bookies or women, had taught him how comforting it was to tell your sad story to a compassionate listener.

'Would it,' he said, 'be impertinent of me, always bearing in mind that your father and I were old friends and that I may quite possibly have dandled you on my knee as a baby, if I asked what caused the rift between you and young Sandy?'

'Not at all. But it's rather a long story.'

'I have all the time in the world. I've got to meet my brother at Barribault's Hotel, but that's only just round the corner and he won't mind waiting. I'll trickle in, shall I?'

'Do. How about a drink?'

'If you have a spot of whisky?'

'The one thing I do have.'

'Excellent. But I'm afraid I'm interrupting your work.'

'Oh, that's all right. I'm only writing a story about a kitten, and I had got stuck when you arrived. What can I make a kitten do?'

'Chase its tail?'

'But after that? I need a strong story line and a couple of situations that'll knock the *Wee Tots* subscribers' eyes out.'

'Is it your aim to amuse the little blisters, or do you
want to scare the pants off them?'

'Either. I'm not fussy.'

'I'm afraid I can't help you.'

'Then help yourself,' said Sam hospitably, placing
bottle, glass and syphon at his side.

2

Gally took a restorative draught. Refreshed, he lit a
cigarette.

'*Wee Tots,*' he said meditatively. 'I know a fellow who
once edited that powerful sheet. Monty Bodkin. Ever
meet him?'

'I've seen him at the Drones.'

'You are a member of the Drones Club?'

Sam gave a short, bitter laugh.

'Am I a member of the Drones Club! Yes, Mr
Threepwood –'

'Call me Gally.'

'May I?'

'Of course. Everybody does. You were saying – ?'

'Yes, Gally, I am a member of the Drones Club. If I
weren't, there wouldn't have been this trouble between
Sandy and me.'

'She wanted you to resign?'

'No, it wasn't that. But I'd better begin at the
beginning, hadn't I?'

'It sounds an excellent idea.'

Sam mused, marshalling his thoughts. Producing
another glass, he mixed himself a whisky and soda. It
stimulated him to speech.

'Well, the first thing that happened was that I was
rather frank about her spectacles.'

'I don't follow you.'

'I mean that was what really started the

unpleasantness. It got the conversation off on the wrong note. Is she wearing those damned spectacles?'

'Never without them. A pity she's had to take to them. They spoil her appearance.'

'That's what I told her. I said they made her look like a horror from outer space.'

'And what had she to say in response?'

'Oh, this and that,' said Sam. It was plain that the memory was not one on which he cared to dwell.

Gally pursed his lips. He was a chivalrous man. In his time he had said things equally or even more offensive to silver ring bookmakers and their like, but these had invariably been of the male sex. To women from youth upward he had always prided himself on being scrupulously polite. Even on the occasion in his early days when a ballet dancer of mixed Spanish and Italian parentage had stabbed him in the leg with a hatpin, his manner had remained suave and his language guarded.

'You ought not to have taunted her about her physical misfortunes, my boy,' he said disapprovingly. 'She can't help wearing spectacles.'

'But she can. That's the whole point. Her eyesight's perfect. The beastly things are made of plain glass, and she only put them on to impress Lord Emsworth.'

'Her train of thought eludes me.'

'She said they made her look older.'

'Ah yes, I see what she meant. Chet Tipton never objected to her functioning without the headlights, but perhaps she feels that my brother will be more critical. And I don't suppose my sister Hermione would approve of a secretary who looks about eighteen.'

'More like seventeen.'

'Yes, possibly more like seventeen. It's an odd thing, but all girls look seventeen to me nowadays. You'll find that yourself when you get to my age. So she took umbrage?'

'She wasn't too pleased.'

'These redheads are always easily stirred. But surely that was merely a trifling tiff, to be cleared up with a kiss and an apology, not the sort of thing to put a girl permanently off the man she loved?'

'There was more.'

'Tell me more.'

'Well, you see, there's this house of mine . . . When you knew my father, did you ever stay at his house in Sussex?'

'Great Swifts? Dozens of times. Big barracks of a place.'

'Exactly. And costs the earth to keep up. My father left it to me, and I want to sell it.'

'I don't blame you.'

'So that I can buy a partnership in a publishing firm. I don't think I've much future at the Bar, but I know I would be sensational as a publisher.'

'There's money in publishing.'

'You bet there is, and I want some of it.'

Gally sipped his whisky thoughtfully. It was unpleasant to have to discourage his young friend's fresh enthusiasms, but he felt it was only kind to warn him that what he was contemplating was far from being the dead snip he seemed to suppose it. England, he knew, was full of landed proprietors anxious to unload their holdings but unable to find takers.

'It may not be too easy to sell it. People these days haven't much use for a big place like that.'

'Oofy has.'

'Who?'

'Oofy Prosser, one of the fellows at the Drones. He's just got married and his wife wants a country house not far from London. She's seen Great Swifts and is crazy about it.'

'That sounds promising. He is rich, this Prosser?'

'Got the stuff in sackfuls. His father was Prosser's Pep Pill; I'm sure I can stick him for at least twenty thousand pounds if the deal goes through.'

Gally's doubts vanished. He had erred, he felt, in supposing the thing not to be a snip.

'Well, as my brother Clarence is so fond of saying, Capital, capital, capital!' Gally paused. He had noted a look of gloom on his companion's face, and it surprised him that he should be despondent when his prospects were so glittering. 'If you don't think it capital, *why* don't you think it capital?'

'Because there's a snag. Oofy insists on having the place done up before he'll part with a cheque. It's rather run down.'

'It was a little that way in your father's time. Buckets in most of the rooms to catch the water coming through the roof and the whole outfit a good deal bitten by mice. I begin to see your difficulty. Will it cost a lot to have it done up?'

'I think I could manage with about seven hundred pounds. But so far I've only been able to save two hundred.'

'Nobody you could touch for the rest?'

'Not a soul. Well, that was the position of affairs when this thing at the Drones happened.'

'You're going too fast for me. What thing at the Drones?'

'The sweep. They had a sweep there.'

'On the Derby?'

'No, on which member of the club would be the next to get married. I suppose it was Oofy's marriage that gave them the idea.'

'A very sound idea. We had a similar sweep at the Pelican years ago, only there it was on who would be the next to die.'

'Rather gruesome.'

'Oh, we didn't mind that at the Pelican. The suggestion was enthusiastically welcomed. The favourite, of course, was old Charlie Pemberton, who was pushing ninety and was known to have had sclerosis of the liver since his early days in the Federated Malay States. I remember how elated your father was when he drew his name out of the hat. He thought he had it made. But, as so often happens, the race went to a dark horse. Buffy Struggles, poor fellow. Got run over by a hansom cab the very day after the drawing. The rankest possible outsider. But I'm interrupting your story. This sweep, you were saying?'

'Well, of course I entered for it.'

'Of course,' said Gally, surprised that any other action should be considered possible. 'How much were the tickets?'

'Ten pounds.'

'Ten *pounds*? Shillings, you must mean.'

'No, pounds. It happened to be at a time when there was an unusual lot of money about. So I put up my tenner, and Sandy gave me the devil. She said it was just throwing it away. She had been a bit austere a few weeks previously when, hoping to bump up my little savings, I speculated on the races and dropped twenty quid.'

Gally nodded. He thought he could see where the narrative was heading.

'And your ten went down the drain and she said "I told you so"?'

'No, I had the most amazing luck. There were only two entries really in the running – Austin Phelps, the tennis player, you've probably heard of him, his name's always in the papers, and Tipton Plimsoll, an American fellow. He's engaged to a girl called Something Wedge.'

'Veronica Wedge. My niece. So you know our Tipton?'

'No, we've never met. We don't even know each other by sight. He's mostly in America and hardly ever comes to the club. He's in America now, but I understand he's coming over here very soon and the wedding will take place directly he arrives.'

'That's right. It's fixed for early in September. Big affair. It'll be at Blandings, with the whole county at the reception.'

'Oh? Well, naturally, when I drew the Plimsoll ticket and heard next day that Phelp's engagement had been broken off for some reason, I thought I was on velvet.'

'And aren't you?'

'It depends on how you look at it. I'm bound to collect the sweep money, which amounts to over five hundred pounds, but I've lost Sandy.'

Gally shook his head.

'I don't get it. I'd have thought she would have flung her arms round you and looked up at you with adoring eyes and murmured "My hero!"'

'You don't know all.'

'How the hell can I if you don't tell me?'

'I'm trying to tell you.'

'Well, get on with it.'

3

Sam refreshed his drink. He was an abstemious young man as a rule, but this morning, possibly because of the disturbances in his love life, possibly because the mere presence of Galahad Threepwood nearly always turned the thoughts of those with whom he forgathered in the direction of alcohol, he felt impelled to indulge. He took a deep draught and resumed.

'She couldn't forgive the stand I took about the syndicate.'

Gally stirred in his chair, exasperated. An accomplished raconteur himself, he chafed when others were obscure. He was thinking that if this was his young friend's customary way of telling a story, it was madness on his part to suppose that anything of his, no matter how strong its kitten interest, would have a chance of acceptance by a discriminating organ like *Wee Tots*. His monocle flashed fire.

'What syndicate? Which syndicate? What do you mean, the syndicate?'

'I was approached by a syndicate,' said Sam, suddenly becoming lucid, 'who offered me a hundred pounds for my Plimsoll ticket.'

Gally started.

'You weren't ass enough to take it?'

'No.'

'Good boy,' said Gally, relieved. 'I thought for a moment you were going to tell me you did.'

Sam scowled at an inoffensive fly which was stropping its back legs on the syphon.

'It might have been better if I had,' he said morosely. 'That was what Sandy and I split up about. She wanted me to close with the offer. Her view was that a sure hundred was money in the bank, while an uncertain five wasn't.'

Gally nodded sagely.

'Women are notoriously deficient in sporting blood. They resent one having a flutter and going for the big stakes. I remember, when I was a kid, someone gave me ten bob on my birthday and influenced by a hot tip from the local hairdresser when he was cutting my hair I planked the entire sum on the nose of a long-priced outsider for the Grand National. You never heard such a fuss as the female members of my family made when the story broke. I couldn't have got nastier notices if I'd been caught burgling the Bank of England. My selection wasn't placed, unfortunately, which made it worse. So what happened?'

'Oh, we argued for hours, and when I remained firm and absolutely refused to take the syndicate offer, she blew her top.'

'Girls with her shade of hair are sadly apt to. I've often wondered why Nature, widely publicized as being infinite in its wisdom, should have made the grave mistake of creating redheads, always so impulsive and quick on the trigger. If she had been a brunette or a platinum blonde, this tragedy would never have occurred. So she gave you back the ring?'

'She threw it at me. You may have noticed the slight abrasion on my left cheek.'

'And now she's returned your letters. All because of your larger vision. All because you very properly saw that more was to be gained by taking a chance. You say you argued for hours. Had her arguments any sense in them?'

Sam had been sorely hurt, but he was fair and could give credit where credit was due.

'Well, yes, I suppose they had in a way. When she was working for his uncle, she saw a lot of this fellow Plimsoll, and she said he was always getting engaged and nothing ever came of it. She said it would be the same with your niece. Apparently girls who get engaged to him have second thoughts.'

'Veronica won't.'

'What makes you so sure of that?'

'The fact that since Sandy knew him his uncle has died, leaving him millions. My sister Hermione will see to it that her ewe lamb doesn't get ideas into her head. You can take it as certain that whatever false starts Tipton Plimsoll may have made in the matrimonial race in the past, this time the wedding is going to come off.'

'Well, that's good, of course, but it doesn't alter the fact that I've lost Sandy.'

'Are you sure she's the right girl for you?'

'Quite sure. No argument about that.'

'Well, I'm not saying you're wrong. I've found her charming, and I suppose she can't help having that feminine streak of caution. The best of girls always want to play it safe. Yes, I think she's the mate for you.'

'But she doesn't.'

'Temporarily, perhaps. But she'll come round. You only have to talk to her quietly and reasonably and she'll be co-operative all right.'

'How can I talk to her? She's at Blandings Castle and I'm in London.'

Gally's eyebrows rose, but such was his personal magnetism that the monocle remained in its place. He stared at Sam incredulously.

'You aren't proposing to remain in London?'

'Where else?'

'My dear boy, have you no spirit, no enterprise? You must take the first train to Market Blandings. I say Market Blandings because I am unfortunately not in a position to invite you to the castle. My sister Hermione is in charge there, and for some reason all my sisters have got the idea that if someone's a friend of mine, he must be a rat of the underworld. No guest of my inviting would last a minute in the dear old place. Hermione would get a grip on his trouser seat and he would find himself flung out on his ear before he had finished unpacking. No, what you do is go to Market Blandings, take a room at the Emsworth Arms and lie in wait. Sandy is always bicycling to Market Blandings to change library books and so on. You're on the watch, and you spring out at her from behind a lamp post and go into your sales talk. Girls like being sprung out at. They take it as a compliment. At your age I was always springing out at girls I'd had some little disagreement with, and it never failed to lead to a peaceful settlement.'

'But suppose she doesn't bicycle to Market Blandings?'

'Then we must arrange a meeting on Visitors' Day.'

'What's that?'

'Thursday of each week is Visitors' Day at the castle.

You cough up half-a-crown and Beach, our butler, shows you round. The battlements, the portrait gallery, the amber drawing-room, all that sort of thing. The customers come from Wolverhampton, Bridgnorth and other centres. All you have to do is join the mob and there you are. The thing's in the bag.'

His enthusiasm began to infect Sam.

'It certainly sounds good,' he agreed. 'But how do I get hold of Sandy?'

'I'll bring her along.'

'Where to?'

'Yes, we must fix a meeting place. We'd better make it the Empress's sty.'

'The what?'

'The residence of Empress of Blandings, my brother's prize pig.'

'Oh, I see. How do I find it?'

'Anyone will tell you where it is. It's one of the Blandings' landmarks. So I may expect you shortly?'

'I'll take a train to Market Blandings this afternoon.'

'That's the way I like to hear you talk. Give me a ring on the telephone when you arrive. And now,' said Gally, 'I must be getting along to Barribault's and picking up Clarence.'

4

Having been carefully informed by Sandy Callender on the telephone the previous evening that he would be calling for him shortly before one and it now being twelve fifty-four, Lord Emsworth was naturally astounded to see Gally. He was sitting in the lounge when Gally reached Barribault's Hotel, his long lean body draped like a wet sock on a chair, and he appeared to be thinking of absolutely nothing. His mild face wore the dazed look it always wore when he was in London, a city that disturbed and bewildered him. Unlike his

younger brother, to whom it had always been an earthly
Paradise, he was allergic to England's metropolis and
counted each minute lost that he was obliged to spend
there. He rose like a snake hurriedly uncoiling itself and
his pince-nez flew from his nose and danced at the end
of their string, their invariable habit when he was
startled.

'God bless my soul! Galahad!'

'In person. Weren't you expecting me?'

'Eh? Oh yes, of course, yes. You're looking very well,
Galahad.'

'You, too, Clarence. Your travels have given you a
sparkle.'

'Have you lunched?'

'What, at my own expense with you all eagerness to
fill me to the brim at yours? Not likely,' said Gally.
'Let's go in, shall we, and as we fortify ourselves for the
drive home you can tell me about your American
adventures – what shows you saw, what bars you were
thrown out of and so on, and I'll give you the latest news
from Blandings.'

Quite a number of his acquaintances, most of them
looking like men whom the police were anxious to
interview because they had reason to believe that they
might be able to assist them in their inquiries, accosted
Gally as he went through the grill-room, and he had a
good deal of stopping and passing the time of the day to
do. It was consequently not for some little while that he
and Lord Emsworth were at their table, dealing with
their orders of sole mornay and able to take up the
thread of their conversation again.

Gally was the first to speak.

'Well, Clarence, what did you think of America?'

'Extraordinary country. You know it well, don't you?'

'Oh yes, I was always popping in and out of it in the
old days. You found it extraordinary, you say?'

'Very. Those tea bags.'

'I beg your pardon?'

'They serve your tea in little bags.'

'So they do. I remember.'

'And when you ask for a boiled egg, they bring it to you mashed up in a glass.'

'You don't like it that way?'

'No, I don't.'

'Then the smart thing to do is not to ask for a boiled egg.'

'True,' said Lord Emsworth, who had not thought of that.

'Though the way things are going now over there, you're lucky if you're able to afford boiled eggs.'

'Eh?'

'Didn't you read in the papers about the crash on the American Stock Exchange?'

'I did not see any papers while I was in New York. They left one outside my door every morning, but I never read it. Has there been a crash on the Stock Exchange?'

'And how! Fellows jumping out of windows in droves. That's America for you. One day you're a millionaire, the next you're selling apples.'

'Selling apples?'

'That's right.'

'Why apples?'

'Why not apples?'

'True. Do you think Constance's husband – I forget his name – is selling apples?'

'I don't imagine so. I remember him telling me his money was mostly in Government bonds. How was the wedding, by the way? Did you get Connie off all right?'

'Yes. Oh yes. They are spending the honeymoon at a town called Cape Cod.'

'I know it well. Cape Cod, the Forbidden City. But something in your eye tells me you don't want to talk about Connie and her nuptials, you want to be brought up to date on the latest happenings at Blandings. Let me think. Well, I suppose the first thing you'll want to hear is how the Empress has been getting on in your absence. You will be relieved to learn that she's as robust as ever, her health all that her friends and well-wishers could desire. Rosy cheeks and sparkling eyes. Under the ministrations of Monica Simmons she has flourished like a green bay tree. You'll be glad to see her again.'

'Yes, yes, oh yes indeed. And it is wonderful to think that Constance will not be there to look disapproving and make clicking noises with her tongue when I go off to the sty. You've no idea how I am looking forward to settling down at Blandings without . . . well, of course nobody could be fonder of Constance than I am, but . . .'

'I get your meaning, Clarence. No need to be apologetic about it. You know and I know that Connie was a Grade A pest.'

'I wouldn't say that.'

'I would.'

'But she was very autocratic.'

'Very. Bossy is perhaps the word.'

'Odd how all our sisters are like that.'

'I've always said it was a mistake to have sisters. We should have set our faces against it from the outset.'

'Constance . . . Dora . . . Julia . . . Hermione . . . How they oppressed me! None of them would ever leave me alone. They were always wanting me to *do* things, always saying I must keep up my position.'

'That's what you get for being the head of the family. We younger sons escape all that sort of thing.'

'Hermione, of course, was the worst of them, but fortunately she was not very often at Blandings, while Constance was there all the time. You never attended the annual school treat, did you, Galahad?'

'Too much sense.'

'Constance always made me wear a top hat for it.'

'I'll bet you were a sensation.'

'And a stiff collar. Yes, I must confess that, devoted as I am to Constance, it will be a wonderful relief to be free from feminine society. The peace of it! By the way, who was that who spoke to me on the telephone yesterday? A strange female voice.'

'You can hardly expect me to keep tab on all the strange female voices that ring you up on the telephone. You know what a dog you are with the other sex.'

Lord Emsworth allowed this innuendo to pass, probably feeling that his reputation needed no defending. Since the death of his wife twenty-five years ago he had made something of a life work of avoiding women. In sharp contradistinction to Gally, who liked nothing better than their society and in his younger days had always been happiest when knee deep in ballet girls and barmaids, he had taken considerable pains to keep them at a distance. He could not hope, of course, to evade them altogether, for women have a nasty way of popping up at unexpected moments, but he was quick on his feet and his policy of suddenly disappearing like a diving duck had had excellent results. It was now pretty generally accepted in his little circle that he was not a ladies' man and that any woman who tried to get a civil word out of him did so at her own risk.

'She was speaking from Blandings. She said you would be coming here today to pick me up. She told me her name . . . now what did she say her name was?'

'Callender. Sandy Callender. She's your secretary.'

'But I have no secretary.'

'Yes, you have.'

'I'm sure you're mistaken, Galahad.'

'No, I'm not. She's your secretary all right. Hermione engaged her.'

Lord Emsworth was a mild man, but he could be roused to wrath.

'Meddlesome and officious!' he cried, his eyes gleaming militantly behind their pince-nez.

'High-handed impertinence! What business has Hermione to engage secretaries for me? When did she do this?'

'Shortly after her arrival at Blandings.'

The sole lay untasted on Lord Emsworth's plate, the hock unsipped in his wine glass. His pince-nez had gone adrift again and his nude eyes glazed at Gally with a horror that touched the latter's heart.

'Hermione's not at Blandings?' he quavered.

Gally patted his hand sympathetically. He knew how he felt.

'I've been wondering all this time how to break it to you, Clarence. I was planning to do it gently, but perhaps the surgeon's knife is best. Yes, Hermione has moved in and is firmly wedged into the woodwork. Egbert's there, too, of course. And Wilfred Allsop.'

'And that tall half-witted girl of theirs?'

'If you are alluding to your niece Veronica, no. She's in London. I brought her with me this morning and left her at Dora's. I gather she's stocking up with clothes against the day when young Plimsoll returns from America and makes her his bride. I'm afraid this has been something of a blow to you, Clarence.'

Lord Emsworth nodded dismally, limp among the ruins of his golden dreams. The prospect of having his sister Hermione substituted for his sister Constance had affected him rather as the announcement that for the future they might expect to be chastised with scorpions instead of, as under the previous administration, with whips must have affected the Children of Israel. Nobody who knew her would have denied that Constance was an able disciplinarian, but they would have been obliged to concede that she could not be considered in Hermione's class. Hermione began where she left off.

'Oh dear, oh dear!' he whispered with bowed head, seeming to be addressing what remained of his sole mornay.

For perhaps a fleeting second Gally hesitated before speaking. It pained his kindly heart to witness his brother's distress, but having adopted the policy of the surgeon's knife he felt that the worst must be told even if it led to the stricken man having what in the land from which he had just returned is known as a conniption fit.

'I wonder, Clarence,' he said, 'if you remember a girl called Daphne Littlewood? And don't think I'm changing the subject, because she is definitely germane to the issue.'

There were very few things that Lord Emsworth ever remembered. This was not one of them.

'Daphne Littlewood? No, I do not.'

'Tall, dark, handsome girl with a formidable personality, not unlike Connie in appearance. In fact, except that she has different coloured eyes and hair, she could go on and play Connie without make-up. She married a rather celebrated historian named Winkworth. She's a widow now with a small and repulsive son and runs a fashionable girls' school. They think a lot of her in educational circles, so much so that she was made a Dame in the last Birthday Honours, a thing that's never likely to happen to you or me. I often wonder who had the idea of calling these women Dames. Probably an American. There's nothing like a dame, he told them, and they agreed with him, and so the order came into being. But I'm wandering from my subject. You've really forgotten Daphne?'

'Completely.'

'Strange. Twenty years ago the bookies were taking bets that you'd get engaged to her.'

'Impossible!'

'That's how the story goes.'

'It is inconceivable that I should have contemplated such a thing.'

'You say that now, but you know what your memory

is like. For all you know, you may have wooed her
ardently – sent her flowers, written in her confession
book, pressed her hand in a conservatory during a dance
. . . No,' said Gally on reflection. 'I doubt if even in your
prime you would have been as licentious as that. Well,
anyway, that's who Daphne Winkworth is, and you'll
find her at Blandings when we get there.'

'What!'

'With her son Huxley. Hermione invited them.'

'Good God!'

'I was afraid it would upset you, and I'm sorry to say
that that's not all. The worst is yet to come.'

Gally paused. He was very fond of Lord Emsworth
and hated to upset him, and he knew that what he was
about to say would make his eyes, like stars, start from
their spheres and also cause his knotted and combined
locks, if you could call them that, to part and each
particular hair – there were about twenty of them – to
stand on end like quills upon the fretful porpentine. He
shrank from saying it, but it had to be said. Impossible
to allow the poor dear old chap to arrive at Blandings
unwarned.

'Hold on to your chair, Clarence, for you're going to
get a nasty shock. Has Hermione brought Dame Daphne
Winkworth to Blandings because they're old friends? No.
Because she enjoys the society of little Huxley
Winkworth? No. Then why, you ask. I'll tell you. It's
because she remembers that old romance and hopes it
may flare up again. I'm not absolutely certain of my
facts, mind you, and it may be that I am alarming you
unnecessarily, but from something Egbert let fall when I
was talking to him last night I received the distinct
impression that she's planning to marry you off this
season.'

'What!'

'And Daphne, I gather, is all for it. She feels that little
Huxley needs a father.'

Lord Emsworth had sunk back in his chair and was looking like the Good Old Man in old-fashioned melodrama when the villain has foreclosed the mortgage on the ancestral farm. There was not a great deal of flesh on his angular form, but what there was was creeping. Over in a corner of the grill-room a luncher was dealing with madrilene soup. It quivered beneath his spoon, but not so wholeheartedly as Lord Emsworth was quivering.

He knew Hermione. His sister Constance had always been able to dominate him and force him into courses against which his whole nature rebelled, like wearing a top hat and a stiff collar at the school treat, and Hermione had twice Constance's determination and will to win. If Galahad was right, the peril that threatened him was appalling and never before had his diving duck technique been so sorely needed. But would even the elusiveness of the diving duck be enough to save him?

'You can't be sure, Galahad,' was all he could find to say.

'I told you I wasn't, but Egbert's remarks seemed to me capable of only one interpretation, and I strongly urge you old man, to be alert and on your guard. Only ceaseless vigilance can save you. Don't let her get you alone in the rose garden or on the terrace by moonlight. If she starts talking about the dear old days, change the subject. On no account pat little Huxley on the head and take him for walks. And above all be wary if she asks you to read her extracts from the *Indian Love Lyrics* after dinner. The advice I would give to every young man starting out in life, and that includes you, though of course it's some time since you started, is to avoid the *Indian Love Lyrics* like poison. I remember poor Puffy Benger, a great pal of mine in the Pelican days, getting irretrievably hooked just because in a careless moment he allowed a girl to lure him into reading *Pale Hands I Loved Beside The Shalimar* to her. And I myself . . . Ah,' said Gally breaking off as he saw the waiter approaching the table. 'Coffee at last. You'll probably need a drop of brandy in yours, Clarence.'

4

It was a little past two o'clock when Gally helped a still
stupefied Lord Emsworth into the car, adjusted his legs,
which always tended to behave like the tentacles of an
octopus when he rode in any conveyance, and started on
the homeward journey, easing his way through the
London traffic with practised skill. At five, Beach, ably
assisted by two footmen, served tea in the amber
drawing-room of Blandings Castle, and the company
awaiting the wanderer's return settled down to keep
body and soul together with buttered toast, cucumber
sandwiches and cake. Lady Hermione Wedge officiated
at the tea pot. Colonel Egbert Wedge stood supporting
his shoulderblades against the mantelpiece over the
fireplace. Dame Daphne Winkworth sat very upright on
what looked an uncomfortable chair, and her son Huxley
perched on a footstool as near as he could get to the
gate-leg table where the food was. Wilfred Allsop was
not present. He was making a point, when possible, of
avoiding Dame Daphne's society. Hers, as Gally had
said, was a formidable personality. It had been so even in
her youth, and many years of conducting a large school
for girls had increased its intensity, giving her an
imperious air calculated to intimidate all but the
toughest. The thought that before many weeks had
passed he would become a member of her staff,
permanently under that eye of hers, never failed to
induce in Wilfred a sinking feeling.

Sandy Callender came in with a slip of paper in her
hand.

'The post office has just telephoned this telegram, Lady Hermione,' she said.

'Oh, thank you, Miss Callender. It is from Tipton, Egbert,' said Lady Hermione as the door closed behind Lord Emsworth's conscientious secretary. 'He has arrived in London and will be coming here tomorrow. Tipton,' she explained to Dame Daphne, 'is the charming young American who is marrying Veronica.'

'Splendid chap,' said Colonel Wedge, whose spirits always rose when he thought of his future son-in-law's millions.

'Yes, we are devoted to dear Tipton. Veronica, of course, adores him.'

'Love at first sight,' said Colonel Wedge. 'Very romantic.'

'He has been in New York, looking after his business interests. He inherited a great deal of money from an uncle.'

'Chester Tipton. Chet, they called him. Galahad used to know him.'

'I wonder if Clarence and he met when he was over there.'

'We must ask him. Ah, that must be Clarence now.'

A tooting had made itself heard from the direction of the front door, and presently footsteps sounded outside. It was not, however, Lord Emsworth who entered, but Beach. His presence surprised Lady Hermione.

'Was that the car, Beach?'

'Yes, m'lady.'

'Then where is Lord Emsworth?'

'His lordship desired me to say that he would be delayed a few moments, as he has gone to see his pig, m'lady,' said Beach and, his mission accomplished, withdrew.

Dame Daphne seemed puzzled.

'Where did he say Clarence had gone?'

'To see his pig,' said Lady Hermione, speaking the final word as if it soiled her lips.

'Prize pig. Empress of Blandings it's called,' Colonel Wedge explained. 'Clarence is crazy about it.'

'That pig needs exercise,' said Huxley, speaking thickly through a mouthful of cake. He was a small, wizened, supercilious boy with a penetrating eye, who had inherited some of the qualities of both his parents – from his mother that air of hers of calm superiority, from his father the sardonic manner which had made him so unpopular in the Common Room of his college at Cambridge. 'Too fat. I'm going to let it out of the sty and make it run.'

And with the feeling that there was no time like the present, he left the room. It had occurred to him that at this hour Monica Simmons might be off somewhere having her cup of tea, and her absence was vital to his plans. He had a wholesome fear of that well-muscled girl, and her statement at their last meeting that if she caught him hanging around the Empress's boudoir again, she would skin him alive had not failed to make an impression on him. It was only when he was half-way down the stairs that he remembered that Lord Emsworth was at the sty, and he decided to give the thing up for the moment. It would, he saw, be necessary to bide his time.

'Crazy,' said Colonel Wedge, continuing his remarks. 'Let me tell you an incident that happened when we were here a year or two ago. I came back late one night from a Loyal Sons of Shropshire dinner in London and went for a stroll in the grounds to stretch my legs after the long train journey, and I was passing the Empress's sty when something I had taken for a suit of overalls hanging on the rail suddenly reared itself up, and it was Clarence. Gave me no end of a start. I asked him what he was doing there at that time of night – it was about twelve o'clock – and he said he was listening to his pig. And what was the pig doing, as I said to Hermione when I talked it over with her later? Singing? Reciting Gunga Din? Not at all. It was just breathing and Clarence was listening to it – courting lumbago, as I told him.'

There had been a frown on Lady Hermione's face as this anecdote proceeded. She was not pleased with her husband for telling a story which might well make Lord Emsworth's destined bride dubious as to the advisability of linking her lot with a man who went out at midnight to listen to pigs breathing. It seemed to her that Dame Daphne was pursing her lips as she might have pursed them in her study at school, had she been informed by an under-mistress that Angela and Phyllis had been found smoking cigarettes behind the gymnasium.

'All it was doing,' said Colonel Wedge, driving home his point in case it might have been missed, 'was breathing. You remember what I said to you, old girl? "Old girl," I said to you, "we've got to face it, Clarence is dotty."'

'Nothing of the kind,' said Lady Hermione sharply, and would have gone on to add that what her brother needed was a wife who would put a stop to all this fussing over a ridiculous pig, when Lord Emsworth made his belated appearance.

'Ah, Hermione,' he said. 'Ah, Egbert. Quite, quite.'

Lady Hermione regarded him austerely. Considering that he was returning from travels which had involved facing all the perils of New York and two ship's concerts, at one of which he had had to take the chair, her greeting might have been more affectionate.

'So here you are at last, Clarence. We had almost given you up. You remember Daphne Winkworth who used to be Daphne Littlewood?'

'Oh, quite. Yes, quite,' said Lord Emsworth.

He spoke with splendid fortitude. There was nothing in his manner or his voice to show that the sight of this woman was making him feel like the hero of a novel of suspense trapped in an underground den by the personnel of the Black Moustache gang. Your English aristocrat learns to wear the mask.

'Daphne is staying with us till her school re-opens.'

'Quite.'

Feeling possibly that if not checked he would go on saying 'Quite' for the rest of the evening, Lady Hermione asked him coldly if he would like some tea and with a final 'Quite' and a 'Tea? Tea? Yes, that would be capital, capital' he sat down and began to sip. Colonel Wedge offered him a hospitable cucumber sandwich.

'Glad to see you again, Clarence,' he said. 'You've caught me just in time. I'm off tomorrow.'

A quick gleam of hope shone on Lord Emsworth's darkness.

'Hermione, too?' he said, feeling that things were looking up.

'Good Lord, no. Hermione isn't coming with me. I shall only be away a day or two. My godmother in Worcestershire, it's her birthday the day after tomorrow, and I always have to be with her for that. Sort of a royal command.'

'Oh?' said Lord Emsworth, his hopes shattered.

He was feeling bewildered. Eyeing Dame Daphne furtively over his cup, he found it incredible that even twenty years ago, when he was younger and sprightlier than he was today and presumably capable of feats of daring now beyond him, he could have contemplated getting engaged to so forbidding a woman. And the thought of actually marrying her made him feel that instead of the cucumber sandwich at which he was nibbling he was swallowing butterflies. He was willing to respect Dame Daphne Winkworth, to wish her continued success in her chosen career and to recommend her seminary to parents with daughters requiring education, but that was as far as he was prepared to go.

He was roused from the coma into which he had fallen by the sound of Dame Daphne's voice. She was saying that she had letters to write. With an unusual glimmering of the social sense he rose and opened the door for her.

'Strange,' he said, returning to his chair. 'Galahad assures me that she and I were acquainted many years ago, but I can honestly say I didn't know her from Eve. What did you tell me her name used to be?'

'Never mind her name,' said Lady Hermione tartly. 'Clarence, you really are impossible.'

'Eh?'

'Going off like that instead of coming here when you arrived.'

'But I wanted to see my pig.'

'No manners whatever. I could see that Daphne was offended. Anyone would have been. I hope you will take the trouble to be more polite to Tipton.'

'Eh?'

'A telegram has come from Tipton saying that he will be here tomorrow.'

'Who is Tipton?'

'Oh, Clarence! Tipton Plimsoll is the man who is marrying Veronica.'

'Who –' Lord Emsworth began, but was able to save himself in time. 'Yes, yes, of course. Your daughter Veronica, you mean. Quite.'

'Did you see anything of Tipton when you were in New York?' asked Colonel Wedge.

An 'Eh? What? No, I didn't,' was trembling on Lord Emsworth's lips, when recollection flooded in on him. Plimsoll. Tipton Plimsoll. Of course, yes. It all came back to him.

'No, we didn't meet,' he said, 'but he rang me up one

night on the telephone. Nice fellow, I thought. Rather a husky voice, but very civil. Too bad he's lost all his money.'

2

It was not often that Lord Emsworth's *obiter dicta* attracted any close attention. People when he spoke were inclined either not to listen to him at all or, if his remarks did reach their ears, to dismiss them as unworthy of their notice. But not even Gally, telling the latest good story to an admiring circle at the Pelican Club, could have gripped his audience more surely than he with these few simple words had done.

There fell upon the room a silence of the kind usually described as stunned. Eyes widened, jaws dropped. Then the Wedges, colonel and wife, spoke simultaneously.

'Done *what*?' cried the colonel.

'Lost his *money*?' cried Lady Hermione.

'Yes, didn't you know?' said Lord Emsworth, mildly surprised. 'I'd have thought he would have told you. He's completely destitute. He's selling apples.'

Lady Hermione clutched her forehead, Colonel Wedge his moustache.

'Apples?' said Lady Hermione in a low voice.

'How do you mean, apples?' said Colonel Wedge.

Lord Emsworth saw that he would have to do some careful explaining.

'According to Galahad, that is what everybody in America is doing now. I could not quite follow what he was telling me, but as far as I could gather there has been what is called a crash on the Stock Exchange. What that is I'm afraid I don't know, but apparently it is something that causes people to lose money, and when they have lost all their money, they sell apples. Oddly enough, though most people like them, I have never been very fond of apples. Still, they are said to keep the doctor away, so no doubt there is a market for them. I suppose your friends tell you how much to charge. I wouldn't know myself, but Tipton has probably found someone who understands these things. One would sell them by the pound, I imagine, but –'

'Clarence!'

'Eh?'

'Where did you hear this?'

'Hear what?'

'About Tipton losing his money.'

'He told me himself. I remember the conversation quite distinctly. It took place, as I say, on the telephone. All these New York hotels have telephones in the bedrooms. You order your meals through them. A very obliging housemaid told me that. She said that if I wanted let us say breakfast, all I had to do was to pick up the telephone and ask for Room Service, and she was perfectly right, too. I tried it several times and always with success. Did you know that when you order tea in America, they bring it to you in little bags?'

Lady Hermione did not strike her brother with a bludgeon, but this was simply because she had no bludgeon.

'Clarence!'

'Eh?'

'Stop *rambling*!'

'Yes, tell us about this conversation you had with Tipton,' said Colonel Wedge.

'I *am* telling you,' said Lord Emsworth, aggrieved. 'As I was saying, it took place on the telephone. It was very late at night, and I had gone to bed, and suddenly the telephone rang and a voice said "Is that Lord Emsworth?" No, I'm wrong. It said "Hello" and *then* it asked if I was Lord Emsworth. Of course I was, so I said so and it said it was sorry to disturb me at this time of night. "Quite all right, my dear fellow," I said. As a matter of fact, I wasn't asleep. Somebody else had woken me a short while before, another mysterious voice. It wanted to know if I was the Oil of Emsworth, and when I said I was, it rang off. Rather odd, I thought, but I suppose that sort of thing is happening all the time in America. Very strange country.'

'Clarence!'

'Eh?'

'Will you *please* stop dithering and get on with your story.'

'My story? Ah yes. Yes, yes, quite. Where had I got to? Ah yes. This voice – the second voice – said it was sorry to disturb me at this time of night and I said "Quite all right, my dear fellow" or it may have been "Perfectly all right, my dear fellow. By the way, who are you?" I said, and he said he was Tipton Plimsoll. "I've lost all my money" he said, and I said I was sorry to hear that, and he asked me if I would lend him twenty dollars. I forget what this is in our currency, but something quite small, so I said of course I would. I should mention that he had begun by telling me that he was the man who was engaged to my niece Veronica and that he had actually stayed at the castle, though I have no recollection of it. Well, to cut a long story short, I said of course I would, and he thanked me profusely and burst into song.'

It was some minutes since Lady Hermione had clutched her forehead. She repaired this omission.

'*Song?*'

'Yes, he began singing. Something, if I remember, about there being a rainbow in the sky, so let's have another cup of coffee and let's have another piece of pie. I wasn't at all surprised. I suppose it was a long time since he had had a square meal, and pie is very filling. They eat cheese with pie in America, which no doubt is all right for those who like it, but I wouldn't care to do it myself. Well, I asked him if he would be calling for the money in the morning, but he said no, he needed it at once. They're like that over there. Hustle, bustle, do it

now. He said would I send it by messenger, and I said
certainly, and I heard him asking someone called
Garroway what was the address of the prison where he
was.'

'*Prison?*'

'This Garroway seems to have been a knowledgeable
chap, for he told him all right. Galahad used to know a
policeman named Garroway, but he died years ago, so it
can't have been him. Or he? I remember being rapped on
the knuckles by that governess we had when we were
children, Hermione, some name like Biggs or
Postlethwaite, because I couldn't get that he-him thing
right. Yes, apparently he was in custody.'

Lady Hermione had stopped clutching her forehead,
probably feeling that it was using up energy and getting
her nowhere. She was looking like a cook who on the
night of the big dinner party suddenly discovered that
the fishmonger has not sent the lobsters. Her immediate
impulse was to scream, but she forced herself to speak
quietly, and if her voice bore a close resemblance to a
voice from the tomb, the most censorious critic can
hardly blame her.

'Clarence, is this a joke?'

'It can't have been much of a joke for Plimsoll.
Nobody likes having to plead for money.'

'I mean, are you making up all this?'

Lord Emsworth was justly offended. It was difficult
for a man as lean and limp as he was to bridle, but he
came as near to bridling as was within the scope of his
powers.

'Of course I'm not making it up. Why would I make it
up? And how could I if I wanted to? Dash it, do you
think I'm capable of making up a story like that? I'm not
Shakespeare.'

'But how can he have been in prison?'

The question surprised Lord Emsworth.

'Well, lots of fellows do go to prison. Galahad in his

younger days frequently spent the night at Bow Street and if I'm not mistaken once nearly did fourteen days without the option of a fine. He was arrested so often that he tells me he got to know most of the policemen in the West End of London by their first names. Extraordinary names some of them had, too. One of them was called Egbert. Why, bless my soul, Egbert, that's your name, isn't it? Shows what a small world it is.'

Too small, Lady Hermione was thinking, to be large enough to contain with anything like comfort her brother Clarence and herself. Lord Emsworth in one of his rambling moods never failed to affect her powerfully. She hoped she was a charitable woman, but the best she could find to say about the ninth Earl at this juncture was that he did not wear a monocle.

'Good God!' said Colonel Wedge, and this seemed to sum the situation up.

It was growing dark now and as always when the light began to fade his study and his Whipple *On The Care Of The Pig* called to Lord Emsworth. He edged towards the door, and such was the preoccupation his tale had caused that he was through it and down the stairs before his sister or his brother-in-law had observed his going. Years of sliding away from the other sex had given him a technique second to none.

3

In the room he had left, silence, for some moments, hung like a pall. It was as if his simple narrative of night life in New York had robbed its occupants of speech. Lady Hermione's vocal chords were the first to recover.

'Egbert!'

'Yes, old girl?'

'Do you think this is true?'

'Must be, I'm afraid.'

'You know how Clarence gets things muddled up.'

'He does, I agree. As a rule, I write off anything he tells me as just babble from the padded cell. Normally, I wouldn't take Clarence's unsupported word if I saw the countryside flooded and he told me it had been raining. But in this case I don't see how we can doubt. I mean to say, Tipton told him himself.'

'Yes.'

'And touched him for twenty dollars.'

'Yes.'

'Well, there you are, then. Obviously he had been speculating on the Stock Exchange and the crash wiped him out. He isn't the first millionaire that's happened to, and I don't suppose he'll be the last.'

A gloomy silence fell. Colonel Wedge cleared his throat.

'What steps do you propose to take, old girl?'

'Veronica must be told.'

'Of course. Can't have her going blindly into marriage and having the bridegroom reveal to her in the vestry that he hasn't a bean.'

Lady Hermione frowned. She considered that her husband was showing a lack of tact. These military men often do.

'Money has nothing to do with it,' she said. 'If it were simply a matter of Tipton not being as rich as we had supposed, I would have nothing to say. But Clarence says he was in prison.'

'I wonder what they jugged him for.'

'Vagrancy probably or begging in the streets. What does it matter? The point is that we cannot allow Veronica to marry a man with a prison record.'

'So you'll write to Vee?'

'I shall go and see her.'

'Yes, that's the best plan.'

'Ring for Beach and tell him to tell Voules to have the car ready as quickly as possible. He must drive me to London tonight.'

'You'll get there pretty late.'

'Too late, of course, to see her, but I will talk to her in the morning and tell her she must write to Tipton breaking the engagement.'

'Do you think she will?'

'Of course she will. I shall see to that. Veronica always does what I tell her.'

'That's true,' said Colonel Wedge, who resembled his daughter in this respect.

He stepped to the wall and pressed the bell.

5

1

The little country town of Market Blandings is one at
which Shropshire points with pride, and not without
reason. Its decorous High Street, its lichened church, its
red-roofed shops and its age-old inns with their second
storeys bulging comfortably over the pavements
combine to charm the eye, and this is particularly so if
that eye has been accustomed to look daily on Halsey
Court, London W1.

To Sam the place had appealed aesthetically
immediately on his arrival, and on the following
afternoon, as he sat with pad and pencil in the garden of
the Emsworth Arms, he found its spell was being of
great assistance to him professionally. It is a fact well
known to all authors that there is nothing like a change
of scene for stimulating the powers of invention. At
Halsey Chambers Sam had had no success as a
chronicler of the adventures of Pinky-Poo the kitten, but
now he found the stuff simply flowing out. It was not
long before he was able to write 'The End' with the
satisfactory feeling, that, provided the editor was not
suffering from softening of the brain, always an
occupational risk with editors, a cheque from *Wee Tots*
was to all intents and purposes in his pocket.

His task done, his thoughts, like those of every
author who has completed a testing bit of work, turned
in the direction of beer. At dinner on the previous night
and again at lunch he had tried out that of the Emsworth
Arms and found it superb. Rising, he replaced pad and
pencil in his room and made for the bar. And at that

precise moment Beach the butler, looking hot and exhausted, tottered into it.

His duties at the luncheon table concluded and no further buttling being required of him until the dinner hour, Beach had started ponderously down the long drive of Blandings Castle and carried on through the great gate at the end of it and into the high road. Something approximating to a heat wave was in progress and the sun was very sultry, but though the poet Coward has specifically stressed the advisability of avoiding its ultra-violet ray, it was his intention to walk to the Emsworth Arms, a distance of fully two miles, and in due season to walk back again.

It would have gratified Huxley Winkworth had he known that this athletic feat was the direct result of his critique of the previous morning. His words had stung Beach at the time, for there had been a tactlessness in their candour calculated to wound, but he was a fair-minded man and realized on reflection that the child, though one might frown on his mode of expressing himself, might possibly have been right. His figure *was* perhaps a little too full and in need of streamlining. The sedentary life of a butler is apt to take its toll.

Of his misadventures on the way – the beads of perspiration, the laboured breath, the blister on the right foot – it is not necessary to speak. The historian passes on to the moment when, arriving at the Emsworth Arms, he limped into the bar and licking his lips surreptitiously requested the barmaid to draw him a mug of the beer which Sam had found so palatable. He felt that he had earned it.

The barmaid's name was Marlene Wellbeloved and she was the niece of George Cyril Wellbeloved, Lord Emsworth's former pigman. Beach had never been fond of George Cyril, considering him a low proletarian and worse than that a man with no respect for his social superiors. Word had reached him that on several occasions he had been referred to by this untouchable as 'Old Fatty' and 'that stuffed shirt', and the occasion when the other had addressed him with the frightful words 'Hoy, cocky' was still green in his memory. Nothing in the way of chumminess could ever exist between this degraded ex-pigman and himself, but for Marlene he had a tolerant liking, and when after a few desultory exchanges he took out the silver watch he had won in the darts tournament to see how the time was getting along and she said, 'Oo, Mr Beach, can I look at that?' he readily consented. He unhooked it from his waistcoat and laid it on the counter, well pleased with her girlish interest.

Her reactions were all that could have been desired. She uttered two squeaks and a giggle.

'Why, it's beautiful, Mr Beach!'

'A very handsome trophy.'

'And you really won it playing darts?'

'I was so fortunate.'

'Well, I think it's lovely.'

It was as she was saying You must be terribly good at darts, Mr Beach, and Beach was deprecating her praise with a modest gesture of the hand that Constable Evans of the Market Blandings police force entered the bar. He had parked his bicycle outside and was coming in for a quick one before resuming his rounds. On seeing Beach, he temporarily forgot his mission. At the station house that morning he had heard a good one from his sergeant and he wanted to pass it along.

'Hi, Mr Beach.'

'Good afternoon, Mr Evans.'

'Got a story for you.'

'Indeed.'

'Not for your ears, Marlene. Come outside, Mr Beach.'

They went out together just as Sam reached the doorway. A collision was unavoidable.

'Pardon *me*, sir,' said Beach.

'My fault. Entirely my fault. Sorry, sorry, sorry,' said Sam. He spoke with a gay lilt in his voice, for he was in buoyant and optimistic mood. It was not only the circumstances of having finished his story and seen the last of a kitten he had never been fond of that induced this sense of well-being. His conversation with Gally at Halsey Chambers had stimulated him, as conversations with Gally so often stimulated people. It had left him convinced that he had only to meet Sandy and inaugurate a frank round-table talk and all misunderstandings, if you could call what had passed between them a misunderstanding, would be forgotten. He would say he was sorry he had called her a ginger-haired little fathead, she would say she was sorry she had thrown the ring at him, they would kiss again with tears as the late Alfred, Lord Tennyson had so well put it and everything would be all right once more.

There was no possible doubt in his mind that Gally had been correct in describing the thing as in the bag, and the world was looking good to him. He was loving everyone he met. He had caught only a fleeting glimpse of the obese character with whom he had collided in the doorway, but he was sure he was an awfully nice obese character, once you got to know him. He liked the looks of Constable Evans and also those of Marlene Wellbeloved, whom he now approached with a charming smile and a request that she would let him have a stoup of the elixir for which the Emsworth Arms was so justly famous.

'Nice day,' said Marlene as she filled the order for she was a capital conversationalist. A barmaid has to be as quick as lightning with these good things. They promote a friendly atmosphere and stimulate trade.

'Beautiful,' said Sam with equal cordiality. 'Hullo, has

somebody been giving you a watch? Your birthday is it,
or something?'

Marlene giggled. A most musical sound, Sam thought
it. In the mood he was in he would have been equally
appreciative of a squeaking slate pencil.

'It's Old Fatty's. He won it in the darts tournament.'

'Old Fatty? You mean the gentleman I was dancing
the rumba with just now?'

'My Uncle George always calls him Old Fatty. Uncle
George is terribly funny.'

'I'll bet he keeps one and all in stitches. What's it
doing on the counter?'

'He was showing it to me. He went out because
Constable Evans wanted to tell him a dirty story.'

'What was the story? You don't happen to know?'

'No, I don't.'

'I must get him to tell it to me some time. Yes,' said
Sam, picking it up, 'it's certainly a handsome watch.
Well worth winning even at the expense of having to
play darts, which to my mind is about the lousiest
pastime in the –'

'World' he would have concluded, but the word died
on his lips. The door of the Emsworth Arms bar faced
the road and was always kept open in fine weather, and
passing it, wheeling a bicycle, was a red-haired girl at the
sight of whom all thoughts of beer, watches and
barmaids were wiped from his mind as with a sponge.
He bounded out, calling her name, and she looked round
startled. Then as she saw him her eyes widened and
leaping on her bicycle she rode off, gathering speed as
she went. And Sam, breathing a soft expletive, ran after
her, though with little hope that anything constructive
would result.

As he ran, he was dimly aware of a sound like a steam
whistle in his rear, but he had no leisure to give it his
attention.

2

The steam-whistle-like sound which had made so little
impression on Sam had proceeded from the lips of
Marlene Wellbeloved. It had taken her a few seconds to
run to the door and come on the air, for astonishment
had held her momentarily paralysed. Hers until now had
been a placid existence, and nothing like this theft of
valuable watches beneath her very eyes had ever marred
its even tenor. The bar of the Emsworth Arms was not
one of your Malemute saloons where anything may
happen when a bunch of the boys start whooping it up.
Its clients were of the respectable stamp of Beach the
butler, Jno. Robinson, proprietor of the station taxi cab,
and Percy Bulstrode the chemist. It was the first time
that Dangerous Dan McGrews like the customer who
had just left had swum into her ken.

She was, accordingly, deprived of speech. Then, her
vocal cords in mid-season form again, she expressed her
concern and agitation with an EEEEEEEEEEE!! which
probably made itself heard and excited interest in many
a distant parish.

It certainly interested Beach and Constable Evans,
chuckling over the sergeant's story some dozen yards
away. Her voice came to them like a bugle call to a
couple of war horses. They had seen Sam emerge and
start running along the road, but had thought nothing of
it, attributing his mobility to an appointment suddenly
remembered. When, however, they realized that his
departure had been the cause of Marlene Wellbeloved
going EEEEEEEEEEE!! reason told them that there
was something sinister afoot. Level-headed girls like
Marlene do not go EEEEEEEEEEE!! without solid
grounds for doing so. With one accord they ran towards
her, the constable in the lead, Beach, who was not built
for speed, lying a length or two behind.

'Smatter?' asked P. C. Evans, always a man of few
words. A trained observer, he noticed that Marlene was
wringing her hands, and he found the gesture significant.
Coming on top of that EEEEEEEEEEEE!!, it seemed to
P. C. Evans that it meant something.

'Oh, Mr Beach! Oh, Mr Beach!'

'What is it, Miss Wellbeloved?'

'That feller's gone off with your watch!' cried
Marlene, her hands continuing to gyrate. 'He put it in
his pocket and ran off with it!'

The effect of these words on the two men differed
substantially. They froze Beach into a statue of dismay,
for his watch was very dear to him and the bereavement
made him feel like one of those nineteenth century
poets who were always losing dear gazelles. He had not
experienced such a sense of desolation and horror since
the night when a dinner guest at the castle had asked for
a little water to put in his claret. It made him wonder
what the world was coming to.

Constable Evans, on the other hand, had found in her
statement all the uplifting properties of some widely
advertised tonic. Where Beach mourned, he rejoiced. The
cross which all English country policemen have to bear
is the lack of spirit and initiative in the local criminal
classes. A man like New York's Officer Garroway has
always more dope pushers and heist guys and fiends
with hatchet slaying six at his disposal than he knows
what to do with, but in Market Blandings you were
lucky if you got an occasional dog without a collar or
Saturday night drunk and disorderly. It was months
since Constable Evans had made a decent pinch, and this
sudden outbreak of crime brought out all the best in
him. To leap on his machine and begin peddling like a
contestant in a six-day bicycle race was with him the
work of an instant. He did not even stop to say 'Ho', his
customary comment on the unusual.

It was not long before he sighted the man wanted by the police. Sam had soon given up the chase, realizing the futility of trying to overtake on foot a cyclist who had had fifty yards' start. He was standing now in the middle of the road, his lips moving in a silent soliloquy which, if audible, would have had no chance of passing the censors even in these free-speaking days.

The sunny mood in which he had begun the day had changed completely. Five minutes before, he had been the little friend of all the world and could have stepped straight into a Dickens' novel and no questions asked, but now he viewed the human race with a jaundiced eye and could see no future for it. When Constable Evans came riding up, he thought he had never beheld a police officer he liked the looks of less. The man seemed to him to have not a single quality to recommend him to critical approval.

Nor did the constable appear to be liking him. It would have taken a very poor physiognomist to have read into his glance anything even remotely resembling affection. He had a face that seemed to have been carved from some durable substance like granite, and it was with a baleful glitter in his eye that he lowered his bicycle to the ground. As he advanced on Sam, a traveller in the East who knew his tigers of the jungle would have been struck by his resemblance to one of them about to leap on its prey.

'Ho!' he said.

The correct response to this would of course have been a civil 'Ho to you,' but Sam was too preoccupied with his gloomy thoughts to make it. He stared bleakly at Constable Evans. He was at a loss to know why this flatty had thrust his society on him, and he resented his presence.

'Well?' he said briefly, speaking from between clenched teeth. 'What do *you* want?'

'You,' said the constable even more briefly. 'What are you doing with that watch?'

'What watch?'

'This watch,' said Constable Evans, and deftly removed it from the right hand pocket of Sam's coat by the chain which dangled from it.

Sam stared as, when a child, he had so often stared at a conjurer who had just produced from a borrowed top hat two rabbits and a bowl of goldfish.

'Good Lord!' he said. 'That belongs to the fat man at the Emsworth Arms.'

'You're right it belongs to the fat man at the Emsworth Arms.'

'I took it away by mistake.'

Constable Evans was a man who did not laugh readily. Even at the sergeant's anecdote, droll though it was, he had merely smiled. But this drew a quick guffaw from him, and having guffawed he sneered. Another man would have said, 'A likely story!' He merely said, 'Ho!'

Sam saw that explanations were in order.

'What happened was this. The girl behind the bar was showing it to me, and I suddenly saw someone – er – someone I wanted to have a word with pass the door, so I ran out.'

'With the watch in your pocket.'

'I must have put it there without knowing.'

'Ho!'

Remorse for having inadvertently deprived a good man of what was no doubt a treasured possession had calmed Sam down a little. He still felt hostile to the human race and would have been glad to do without it, but he could see that he had put himself in the wrong and would have to make apologies. He clicked his tongue self-reproachfully.

'Idiotic of me. I'll take it back to the owner.'

'*I'll* take it back to the owner.'

'Will you? That's very nice of you. He'll be amused. You'll have a good laugh together.'

'Ho!'

The monosyllable intensified the dislike which Sam had been feeling from the first for this intrusive bluebottle.

'Can't you say anything except Ho?' he snapped.

'Yus,' said Constable Evans. He was not as a rule a quick man with a repartee, but it was not often that he was given an opening like this. With the insufferably complacent air of a comedian who has been fed the line by his straight man he proceeded. 'Yus, I *can* say something except Ho. I can say "You're pinched",' he said, and laid a heavy hand on Sam's shoulder.

It was not the moment to lay hands on Sam's shoulder. He had been finding it difficult enough to endure the conversation of one who seemed to him to combine in his single person all the least attractive qualities of a race – the human – which he particularly disliked, and to have his collarbone massaged by him was, if one may coin a phrase, the last straw. With a reflex action which would have interested Doctor Pavlov his fist shot out and there was a chunky sound as it impinged on the constable's eye with all the weight of his muscular body behind it. It sent him staggering back, his foot tripped over a loose stone and he fell with a crash loud enough for two constables. And Sam, leaping at the bicycle, flung himself on it and rode off at a speed which Beach in his hot youth might have equalled but could not have surpassed. Had he been alive forty years before and a member of the choir attended by Beach, and had his voice by some lucky chance not broken before the first Sunday in Epiphany, thus enabling him to enter for the contest in which the butler had won his spectacular triumph, the race in all probability would have ended in a dead heat.

3

If you start two hundred yards or so from Market Blandings on a bicycle you have stolen from one of the local police force and continue to pedal along the high road, you come before long to the little hamlet of Blandings Parva, which lies at the gates of Blandings Castle. It consists of a few cottages, a church, a vicarage, a general store, a pond with ducks on it, a filling station (its only concession to modernity) and the Blue Boar Inn. The last named was where Sam's trip came to an end.

It was on foot that he completed its final stages, for some time before he reached Blandings Parva the thought had crossed his mind that the sooner he got rid of his Arab steed the better. It is never wise to remain for long in possession of a hot bicycle, particularly one formerly the property of a member of the constabulary. Some quarter of a mile before journey's end, accordingly, he propped the machine against a stile at the side of the road and was able to enter the premises of the Blue Boar in the guise of a blameless hiker. He took a seat in the cool, dim taproom and started to review the situation in which he found himself.

It fell, he immediately perceived, into the category of situations which may be described as not so good. Try to gloss over the facts though he might, he could not reach any conclusion other than that he was a fugitive from justice and one jump, if that, ahead of the police. Totting up the various crimes he had committed – watch stealing, bicycle stealing, resisting an officer in the execution of his duty and causing him bodily injury – he had the feeling that if he got off with a life sentence, he would be lucky.

The problem of what to do next was one beyond his power of solution. It called for a wiser head than his, and most fortunately there was just such a head within easy reach.

'I wonder if you could let me have a piece of paper and an envelope,' he said to the landlord. 'And is there someone who could take a note for me to Mr Galahad Threepwood at the castle?'

The landlord said his son Gary would be happy to, if sixpence changed hands.

'I'll give him a shilling,' said Sam.

He was not a rich man and a shilling was a shilling to him, but if a shilling would provide for him a conference with one for whose ingenuity and resource he had come to feel a profound respect, it would in his opinion be a shilling well spent.

6

I

A night's rest and a strengthening cocktail before lunch had quite dispelled any fatigue Gally might have been feeling as the result of his yesterday's motoring. His superb health, fostered by tobacco, late hours and alcohol, always enabled him to recuperate quickly, and he could be alert and bubbling with energy after activities which would have sent most teetotallers tottering off to their armchairs, to lie limply in them with their feet up.

Sam's telephone call just before lunch, announcing his arrival at the Emsworth Arms, had completed his sense of well being, and he was about to seek Sandy out and tell her of the treat in store for her, when as he passed the door of Lord Emsworth's study it flew open and its occupant came out, his face contorted, his pince-nez flying in the breeze, his whole demeanour that of a man who has been pushed too far.

'Galahad,' he cried passionately, 'I won't stand it. I shall assert myself. I shall take a firm line.'

'Take two if you wish, my dear fellow,' said Gally equably. 'This is Liberty Hall. What are you planning to take firm lines about?'

'This Callender girl. She's driving me mad. She's an insufferable pest. She's worse than Baxter.'

These were strong words. It had always been Lord Emsworth's opinion that the Efficient Baxter, now happily in the employment of an American millionaire and three thousand miles away in Pittsburgh, Pennsylvania, had, when it came to irritating, harrying

and generally oppressing him, set a mark at which all
other secretaries would shoot in vain.

'She's worse than the Briggs woman.'

Here, too, was an impressive statement. Lavender
Briggs, who had resigned her portfolio and gone to
London to conduct a typewriting agency, may not have
been as intolerable as Rupert Baxter, but she had come
very close to achieving that difficult feat.

'She covers my desk with letters which she says I
must answer immediately. She keeps producing them
like a dashed dog bringing his dashed bones into the
dinning-room. Where she digs them out from I can't
imagine. Piles and piles of them.'

'Fan mail, do you think?'

'And what she has done to my study! It stinks of
disinfectant and I can't find a thing.'

'Yes, I saw her tidying it up.'

'Messing it up, you mean. It's hard,' said Lord
Emsworth, quivering with self-pity. 'I go to America to
attend a sister's wedding, and when I come back
expecting to have a little peace at last, what do I find? I
find not only that another sister has come to stay but
that she has introduced into my home a spectacled girl
with red hair whose object seems to be to give me a
nervous breakdown.'

Gally nodded sympathetically. There was nothing he
could do to soothe, but he put in a mild word on Sandy's
behalf.

'It's just zeal, Clarence. You get it in the young. She's
a trier.'

'*I* find her trying,' Lord Emsworth retorted, one of the
most brilliant things he had ever said. It was so good
that he repeated it, and Gally gave another sympathetic
nod.

'I can understand that her ministrations must be hard
to bear,' he said, 'but put yourself in her place. She's a

young girl eager to make good. She's told by her agency
or whatever they call those concerns that they've found
a job for her at Blandings Castle, and her eyes widen.
"Isn't that where the great Lord Emsworth hangs out?"
she says. "Quite correct," they say. She quivers from
head to foot and a startled cry escapes her. "Hell's
bells!" she says. "Then I'll have to spit on my hands and
pull up my socks and leave no stone unturned or my
name will be mud. That boy will expect good service."
What you've got to realize, Clarence, is that you're a
godlike figure to young Sandy. She has heard about you
in legend and song. You awe her. She looks on you as a
cross between a Sultan of the old school and a
grandfather.'

'Grandfather?' said Lord Emsworth, stung.

'Great-grandfather,' said Gally, correcting himself.
'Well, if she has given you all that homework to do,
you'd better buckle down to it.'

'I'm going to see my pig.'

'I'll come with you. I often say there is nothing so
bracing as a good after-luncheon look at the Empress.
Well known Harley Street physicians recommend it. But
you'll catch it from her if she finds you've been playing
hooky.'

'I do not allow myself to be dictated to by my
secretary,' said Lord Emsworth haughtily.

As they made their way to the buttercup-dabbled
meadow in a corner of which the Empress's
self-contained flat was situated, Gally enlivened their
progress with the story of the girl who said to her
betrothed, 'I will not be dictated to!' and then went and
got a job as a stenographer, while Lord Emsworth, who
never listened to stories and very seldom to anything
else, continued to explain why he found Sandy Callender
such a thorn in the flesh. They had reached their
destination and were gazing with suitable reverence on

the silver medallist's superb contours, when a voice
hailed them and, turning, they perceived a long, thin
young man approaching. To Lord Emsworth, though
they had frequently met, he appeared a total stranger and
he merely blinked inquiringly, but Gally, having a better
memory for faces, recognized him as Tipton Plimsoll
and gave him a cheery greeting. He had always been fond
of Tipton, sometimes going so far as to feel that, if that
famous club had still existed, he would have been
perfectly willing to put him up for membership at the
old Pelican.

'Well, when did you get here, Tipton?' he said.

'Hello, Mr Threepwood. I've just arrived. Hello, Lord
Emsworth. They told me in the house they thought you
might be out here. You don't happen to know if Vee's
around?'

The name conveyed nothing to Lord Emsworth.

'Vee? Vee?'

'She's in London,' said Gally.

'Oh, shoot. When do you expect her back?'

'I really couldn't say. I understand she's buying
clothes, so I doubt if you can hope to see her for some
little time. Still, you've always got me. Did you have a
good trip?'

'Swell, thanks.'

'You're looking very bobbish.'

'I'm fine, thanks.'

It seemed to Lord Emsworth that for a man who had
so recently been reduced to beggary by losses on the
Stock Exchange this Tipton, whom with a powerful
effort of the memory he had now recognized, was
extraordinarily buoyant, and he honoured him for his
courage and resilience. He was reminded of a Kipling
poem the curate had recited at a village entertainment
his sister Constance had once made him attend –
something about if you can something something and

never something something, you'll be a man, my son, or words to that effect.

'How was the coffee, Tipton?' he said.

'Pull yourself together, Clarence,' said Gally. 'You're dithering.'

'I am doing nothing of the sort,' said Lord Emsworth warmly. 'We had a most interesting conversation on the telephone one night in New York, and he told me that he was going to have a cup of coffee and a piece of pie.'

'Oh, sure, yes, I remember,' said Tipton. 'And talking of that, I owe you twenty dollars.'

'My dear fellow!'

'I'll give you a cheque when I get back to the house.'

Lord Emsworth was horrified.

'No, really, you must not dream of it. I am amply provided with funds and you cannot possibly afford it. Let us forget the whole thing. Tipton,' he explained to Gally, 'has lost all his money on the Stock Exchange.'

Gally looked grave. As has been said, he liked Tipton and wished him well, and being familiar with his sister Hermione's prejudice against penniless aspirants for her daughter's hand he feared that this was going to affect his matrimonial plans to no little extent. Like so many mothers, Lady Hermione expected a son-in-law to ante up and contribute largely to the kitty.

'Is this true?' he asked, concerned.

Tipton laughed amusedly.

'No, of course it isn't. I'm afraid I misled Lord Emsworth that night in New York. I've never lost a nickel in the market. All I wanted was twenty bucks to get self and friend out of the pokey. Somebody had got away with my roll, leaving me without a cent, and a cop told me bail could be arranged if somebody would loan me the needful. So I thought of Lord Emsworth.'

Illumination came to Gally, and with it a renewed feeling that this young man would have been just the sort of new blood the Pelican would have welcomed.

'Oh, you had been pinched?'

'That's right.'

'Drunk and disorderly?'

'That's right.'

'I see.' A wave of nostalgia flooded over Gally as his thoughts went back to the time when he, too, had lived in Arcady. 'I was always getting pinched for d. and d. myself in my younger days. This was especially so when I supped at the old Gardenia – pulled down now, I regret to say, to make room for a Baptist chapel of all things. I was more or less of a marked man there. The bouncers used to fight for the privilege of throwing me out, and there seldom failed to be a couple of the gendarmerie waiting in the street as I shot through the door, on me like wolves and intensely sceptical of my sobriety. I always felt I was slipping in those days if it didn't take two of them to get me to the police bin, with another walking behind carrying my hat. How are the prisons in New York? I have visited that great city constantly, but oddly enough I was never arrested there. Much the same as on this side, I imagine. The place not to get jugged in is Paris, where similar establishments have no home comforts whatsoever. I remember on one occasion, after a rather sprightly do at the Bal Bullier –'

He was unable to complete what would no doubt have been a diverting anecdote full of inspiring hints for the younger generation, for at this moment a stalwart figure in smock and trousers came striding up. Monica Simmons back from lunch. She greeted her employer with a hearty bellow which echoed over hill and dale.

'Heard you'd arrived, Lord Emsworth,' she boomed. 'Glad to be back, I shouldn't wonder. No place like home, I often say. How do you think the piggy-wiggy's looking?'

'Capital, capital,' said Lord Emsworth. 'Capital, capital, capital.'

He spoke with genuine enthusiasm. There had been a time when both he and Gally had entertained the gravest doubts as to Monica Simmons's fitness for her high position, due to this habit of hers of referring to the Empress as the piggy-wiggy. As Gally had said, it was the wrong tone and seemed to show that she was too frivolous in her outlook to hold so responsible a post. The girl, he pointed out, who carelessly dismisses a three-times silver medallist at the Shropshire Agricultural Show as a piggy-wiggy today is a girl who may quite easily forget to give the noble animal lunch tomorrow. And according to Augustus Whipple in his monumental work a pig cannot afford to skip meals. If it does not consume daily nourishment amounting to fifty-seven hundred calories, these to consist of proteins four pounds five ounces, carbohydrates twenty-five pounds, it becomes a spent force.

But that was all in the past. The term piggy-wiggy no longer made him wince. Monica Simmons had proved herself a worthy daughter of the agricultural college from which she had graduated and more than equal to the tremendous task of keeping Empress of Blandings up to bursting point.

Nor did her conception of her duties stop at providing her charge with calories. Her next words showed that she had its welfare at heart in other directions.

'Oh, by the way, Lord Emsworth,' she said, 'I nearly forgot to ask you. Who would that boy be? A small boy with a face like a prune run over by a motor bus.'

Lord Emsworth was baffled. He had no solution to offer. It was left to Gally to supply the information. The description, he said, fitted Dame Daphne Winkworth's son Huxley like the paper on the wall and could scarcely have been improved upon by the most meticulous stylist.

'But why do you bring him up?' he asked. 'How has he thrust himself on your attention?'

'He keeps hanging round trying to let the Empress out of her sty.'

'He does that?' cried Lord Emsworth, appalled.

'I caught him at it yesterday and again this morning.'

'The next time he does it, give him a good hard knock.'

'I'll rub his face in the mud.'

'And Sandy Callender will rub yours in the mud, Clarence, if you don't go back and attend to your correspondence,' said Gally. 'Come along. The party's over.'

2

Left alone with Monica Simmons and scanning her with a critical eye, Tipton found a difficulty in detecting those glamorous qualities in her which appeared to make so strong an appeal to Wilfred Allsop. He willingly conceded that if attacked by a mad bull or a gang of youths with switch knives and brass knuckles he would be happy to have her at his side, for the muscles of her brawny arms were obviously strong as iron bands, if not stronger, but as an arouser of the softer emotions he could not see her with a spyglass. He was thinking, indeed, as so many men have thought on meeting their friends' loved ones, that given the choice between linking his lot with hers and going over Niagara Falls in a barrel he would greatly prefer the latter form of unpleasantness.

However, being aware that Wilfred held other views, he prepared to do all that was within his power to further his interests, employing more direct methods than his friend had done. Wilfred, he had gathered from his observations in their mutual cell, had been conducting his wooing on remote control or Patience on a monument lines, and it was a policy of which he

thoroughly disapproved. In matters of the heart he was
solidly in favour of laying cards on the table and talking
turkey. Only so could business result.

'Fat pig, that,' he said by way of easing into the deeper
topic he had in mind.

'The fattest in Shropshire, Herefordshire and South
Wales,' said Monica proudly.

'Not on a diet, I notice.'

'No, sir, you don't catch this piggy-wiggy slimming.
She believes in getting hers and to hell with what it does
to her figure. You're the fellow who's marrying Veronica
Wedge, aren't you?'

'That's me. Plimsoll is the name. Tipton Plimsoll.'

'Monica Simmons at this end.'

'I thought as much. Willie Allsop was speaking to me
of you not long ago.'

'Oh, was he?'

'And in the highest terms, I don't mind telling you.
He gave you a rave notice. He couldn't have gone
over-board more completely if you had been the current
Miss America.'

When it came to blushing, Monica Simmons was
handicapped by the fact that her face was obscured by
the mud inseparable from her chosen walk in life. It is
virtually impossible to retain that schoolgirl complexion
unimpaired if you are looking after pigs all the time.
Even more closely than Sandy Callender when tidying
up Lord Emsworth's study she resembled one of those
sons of toil buried beneath tons of soil of whom Gally
had spoken. Nevertheless, probing beyond the geological
strata Tipton thought he could discern a pinkness. Her
substantial foot, moreover, had begun to trace coy
arabesques on the turf. These phenomena encouraged
him to proceed.

'In fact,' he went on, laying the whole deck of cards on
the table and talking turkey without reserve, 'he loves

you like a ton of bricks and his dearest wish is that you will consent to sign your future correspondence Monica Allsop.'

It was impossible for a girl constructed on Monica's lines to leap like a startled fawn, but she quivered perceptibly. A sound not unlike the Empress's grunt proceeded from her, and her eyes rounded to about the dimensions of standard golf balls. It was some moments before she could speak. When she did, the words came out in a husky whisper.

'I can't believe it!'

'Why not? All pretty straightforward, it seems to me. What's your problem?'

'He's so far above me.'

'Couple of inches shorter, I'd have said.'

'Intellectually, I mean.'

'Who ever told you Willie Allsop had an intellect?'

'He looks so spiritual.'

'So do I, but you can't go by that. He may look spiritual, but you can take it from me that he's a regular guy all right. I've seen him when he was going good, and he's well worth watching. But putting that aside for the moment, what I want to know is what his rating is with you. Where does he stand in your book? How would you react if he asked you to marry him? Would you feel he had the right idea, or would you give him the horse's laugh and say "Drop dead, you little squirt"?'

Beneath the mud Monica Simmons flushed hotly. It was plain that an exposed nerve had been touched.

'He is not a little squirt!'

'Well, that's what he says he is. It was precisely how he described himself when he was talking to me about you. "She's so majestic, and I'm such a little squirt" were his exact words. But you appear to think otherwise, so am I to infer that he'd really have a chance of bringing home the bacon?'

'If you mean would I accept him if he asked me to marry him, yes I would. I'd jump into his arms.'

'Well, I'm not sure I'd advise that. I don't want to seem personal, but you're on the solid side and he's kind of flimsy. You might fracture something. Still, the point, the thing we've been trying to get at, is that your views on the subject of centre-aisleing coincide with his, so that's all right. I'll go and tell him.'

'Will you really?'

'Right away.'

'Oh, Mr Plimsoll!'

'Call me Tipton.'

'Oh, Tipton!'

'Or, rather, Tippy.'

'Oh, Tippy, you're an angel.'

'I'm like Officer Garroway, a buddy of mine whom you haven't met,' said Tipton. 'I started out in life as a Boy Scout, and I can't seem to shake off the habit of doing my day's good deed. And now to find Willie.'

3

It was no easy task to do this, for Wilfred Allsop had been detained on the terrace by Dame Daphne Winkworth. Dame Daphne liked to become acquainted with her staff and she had kept him answering personal questions for a full hour, after which he had gone to his room to bathe his forehead. When he emerged, feeling somewhat better though still weak, the first person he met was Tipton, who had almost decided to give up the search.

There took place, of course, something in the nature of a joyous reunion. It was their first meeting since they had parted with mutual civilities outside the New York police station, and each was thinking how greatly the other's looks had improved in the interim. Tipton's face

then had seemed to Wilfred to be an unwholesome
yellow in colour and to flicker a good deal like an early
silent motion picture, and so had Wilfred's to Tipton.
Even now neither could have entered a beauty
competition with any real confidence of success unless
Officer Garroway had been the sole other contestant, but
there had been a distinct change for the better.

When two friends meet after a separation, the
conversation tends as a rule to begin with inquiries from
both regarding old Joes and Jacks and Jimmys whom
they have seen or not seen anything of lately, but as
Tipton Plimsoll and Wilfred Allsop had met only once
and the only acquaintance they had in common was
Officer Garroway, a few exchanges on the subject of that
golden-hearted city employee were enough to cover
these preliminaries and Tipton was almost immediately
at liberty to get down to those brass tacks to which he
always liked to get down as soon as possible.

'Well, Willie,' he said, going straight to the *res*. 'I've
just been having a chat with the Simmons broad. We had
quite a visit.'

An austere look came into Wilfred's face. He had had
to complain before of Tipton's freedom of speech when
alluding to the girl he worshipped. It was the other's
only fault, but a grave one.

'Would you mind not referring to Miss Simmons as a
broad,' he said coldly.

'Sorry. Slip of the tongue. I should have said I've been
talking to your little serving of peaches and cream, and I
have some rather interesting news to impart. It appears
that you are her dream man.'

'What!'

'That's what she told me. You're ace high with her.
She didn't actually say she would die for one little rose
from your hair, but that was the impression she
conveyed. What she said was that if you asked her to

marry you, she would jump into your arms. I don't see what more you want than that.'

Wilfred stared, gulped and tottered.

'You aren't kidding?'

'No, I'm not, and nor was she. All you've got to do is walk up to her, wipe some of the mud off her face, clasp her in your arms, and you're home.'

The programme, as outlined, plainly attracted Wilfred. Nevertheless he hesitated.

'Clasp her in my arms?'

'And kiss her. Having of course cleaned her up a little first. She needs thoroughly going over with soap and hot water.'

Wilfred shook his head.

'I couldn't do it.'

'Why not?'

'I haven't the nerve.'

Tipton smiled indulgently.

'The very words I said to a girl called Prudence Garland when she urged me to propose to Vee.'

'You mean my cousin Prue?'

'Is she your cousin? Everybody seems to be your cousin.'

'She's my Aunt Dora's daughter. She's married to a man named Lister. Bill Lister. They run a sort of road-house place near Oxford.'

'Yes, I remember they wanted me to put money into it, but I was light on my feet and kept away. Well, she was staying here when I first met Vee, and one day she drew me aside and said "You're in love with Vee, aren't you, Mr Plimsoll?"'

'To which you replied?'

'I didn't reply, because I was busy falling off a wall at the time. We were sitting on the wall of the terrace, and her words gave me such a start that I overbalanced. Returning to my seat, I said I was, and she said Well,

why don't you ask her to marry you, and just like you I
said it couldn't be done, because I hadn't the nerve. And
do you know what she suggested?'

'What?'

'She said that that could be readily adjusted if I had a
good quick snort by way of a send-off.'

'And you did?'

'I did, and it altered the whole set-up. It made a new
man of me and I approached the matter in hand in an
entirely different spirit.'

'You became the dominant male?'

'With bells on.'

'And asked Vee to marry you?'

'Ordered would be a better word. I just gave her her
instructions.'

'What did you actually say?'

'By way of leading into the thing? "My woman!", if I
remember rightly. Yes, that was it. "My woman!" I
thought for a moment of saying "My mate!", but
decided against it because it seemed to me to have too
nautical a ring. But you don't need to worry about the
dialogue. That's a side issue. It's the clasping in arms
and kissing that puts the act across. And I'll tell you
what I'll do for you, Willie. In the glove compartment of
my car there is a well-filled flask. It's yours. Slip it in
your pocket and about five minutes before the kick-off
drain its contents. You'll be surprised.'

For an instant Wilfred Allsop's face lit up, as that of
the poet Shelley whom he so closely resembled must
have done when he suddenly realized that 'blithe spirit'
rhymes with 'near it', not that it does, and another ode
as good as off the assembly line. Then it fell. He fingered
his chin dubiously.

'Can I risk it?'

'No risk involved. It's good Scotch.'

'I was thinking of Dame Daphne Winkworth.'

'Who's she?'

'She runs the school where I'm going to teach music.'

'Of course, yes. You mentioned her that night in New York. But how does she come into it?'

'She's staying here. She would fire me like a shot if she caught me drinking. And while drumming the elements of music into the heads of a bunch of goggle-eyed schoolgirls isn't what I'd call an ideal form of employment, it's a job and carries a salary with it. Do you think I ought to take a chance?'

'You'll never get to first base if you don't. When were you planning to contact Miss Simmons?'

'Tomorrow morning, I thought.'

'I'll tell her to expect you then.'

'Though I'm still nervous about Ma Winkworth.'

'Relax. I'll see that she isn't around. I'll get hold of her and keep her talking.'

'You're a true friend, Tippy.'

'I like to do my bit. That's settled then. Shall we just run through the scenario to make sure you've got it straight?'

'It might be as well.'

'Walk up.'

'Walk up.'

'Clasp in arms.'

'Clasp in arms.'

'Kiss.'

'Kiss.'

'And say "My woman!" It's as easy as falling off a log. You can't miss.'

7

It is never pleasant for a girl to find that she is being followed, and if she has to be followed she would always prefer it not to be by a man who has recently called her a ginger-haired little fathead. Sandy, as she passed through the front door of the castle on her return from Market Blandings, was seething with indignation, resentment and a number of other disagreeable emotions. She was also conscious of a choking sensation. The sight of a Sam Bagshott where no Sam Bagshott should have been had taken her breath away and she was still in the process of recovering it.

The front door opened on a spacious hall, and as she entered it a footman appeared at the other end. He was carrying a coiled-up red rope, and this he hooked to a ring in the wall. He then carried it to the opposite wall and hooked it there. After which, he hung up in prominent positions two printed notices, both on the brusque side. One said:

KINDLY KEEP IN LINE

the other:

NO SMOKING

He then dusted his hands and stepped back with the air of a man who has done a good day's work.

Surprise at these peculiar goings-on made Sandy

momentarily forget Sam and his adhesiveness. She would come back to him later, but in the meantime she wanted to know what all this was about. The footman, when she put this question to him, smiled the indulgent smile of the expert illuminating a novice.

'Visitors' Day, miss.'

'Today?'

'No, miss, tomorrow. Premises thrown open to the public every Thursday. Mr Beach shows them round.'

'Do a lot of them come?'

'This hot weather seems to bring them out like flies. Three charabancs and a girls' school last week.'

'I didn't get here till the Friday, so I missed them.'

'You were lucky,' said the footman, his eyes black. He seemed to be brooding on past horrors. 'Draw that rope tight, Thomas,' he added as another footman entered bearing a sign that read:

KINDLY DO NOT FINGER OBJECTS OF ART

'Last Thursday a couple of hussies climbed over it and sat on that fender as bold as brass.'

A sudden disquieting thought struck Sandy like a blow. Only now did that phrase 'Premises thrown open to the public' come home to her.

'Can *anyone* come on Visitors' Day?'

'Anyone that's got half-a-crown, miss,' said the footman, giving the rope another pull.

There was a thoughtful look on Sandy's face as she made her way to the library, to which she planned to give a thorough straightening and tidying. And indeed she had been provided with food for thought. No doubt Gally would have told Sam about Visitors' Day, and if she knew her Gally would have pointed out to him how admirable an opportunity it provided for invading the castle. And once Sam was in the castle a meeting between them, he being the thrustful young man he was, would be inevitable. He might refrain from smoking, and he might not finger objects of art, but the one thing of which she was certain was that he would not kindly keep in line. It would take more than a mere butler and two footmen to restrain him from roaming at large about the place until he found her.

And she recoiled from the thought of being found by him. She did not want to see him even in the distance. All she asked of him was to stay out of her life. She did not conceal from herself that his absence from it had left a gap in her heart like the excavation for the foundation of a sky-scraper, but that could not be helped. Time would presumably fill it up again, and even if that did not happen a man who had called her the things he had called her at their last meeting was obviously a man she was better without.

Reaching the library, she went about her work, but she did it absently. She dusted books, she tidied papers, but her thoughts were not with them. Her mind was concentrated on the problem of how this distasteful encounter could be avoided. It was as she removed from the coal scuttle a letter addressed to her employer which had somehow managed to find that unusual resting place that the solution came to her, and she hurried to Lord Emsworth's study.

Her arrival there startled Lord Emsworth. He peered at her in quick alarm. She looked to him like a girl who had come to bring him some more letters demanding his instant attention. Unless his eyes deceived him, it was a letter she was holding in her hand. He feared the worst, and her words, when she spoke, were music to his ears.

'I wonder if you could possibly spare me for a day or two, Lord Emsworth,' she said. 'My father is very ill.'

This would have struck old friends like Gally and Tipton Plimsoll as peculiar, knowing as they did that

the late Ernest Callender had passed away shortly before
her eighth birthday, but Lord Emsworth, lacking this
knowledge, tut-tuttered courteously.

'I am sorry,' he said. 'Too bad. Quite.'

'Will it be all right if I go away for a few days?'

'Certainly, certainly, certainly, certainly,' said Lord
Emsworth with perhaps a greater enthusiasm than was
tactful. 'Stay away as long as you like. My
brother-in-law Colonel Wedge is catching some sort of a
train this afternoon, got to go to Sussex or somewhere.
You could drive into Market Blandings in the car. An
excellent idea. Yes, quite.'

'Thank you very much.'

'Not at all, not at all.'

'I'll go and pack my things. Oh, by the way, I found
this letter in the coal scuttle in the library. I think you
should answer it at once.'

Lord Emsworth took the letter gloomily. He was
saying to himself that he had thought as much. If Sandy
Callender's come, he would have said if he had been
more poetic than he was, can letters to be answered at
once be far behind?

2

Gally on returning to the house had wandered off to the
smoking-room and begun to glance through the
illustrated weekly papers. But their pages, filled mostly
with photographs of Society brides who looked like
gangsters' molls and the usual gargoyles who attend
Hunt Balls, failed to grip him, and the thought having
occurred to him that another chat with one whose
conversation he always enjoyed might offer greater
entertainment, he made his way to Lord Emsworth's
study. And he had just reached the door when Lord
Emsworth came popping out like a cuckoo from a
cuckoo clock.

'Oh, Galahad,' he said. 'The very man I was looking for.'

To Gally's surprise he seemed, despite the fact that Blandings Castle had been filling up so much of late, in excellent spirits. On their way to the sty he had been moody and peevish and, when speaking of his current secretary, inclined to wallow in self-pity, but now he was not merely cheerful but exuberantly cheerful.

'Galahad,' he cried, as sunnily as if there had been no Lady Hermione, no Colonel Wedge, no Dame Daphne Winkworth, no little Huxley Winkworth and no Sandy Callender in the house, 'the most wonderful thing has happened. I have never been so pleased in my life.'

'Don't tell me they've made you a Dame?'

'Eh? No, not so far as I know. You told me yourself that such a thing was most unlikely. But you have heard me speak of Augustus Whipple?'

'The chap who wrote that book you're always reading? *Put Me Among The Pigs*, isn't it called?'

'*On The Care Of The Pig*.'

'That's right. Banned in Boston, I believe.'

'Eh?'

'Let it go. What about Augustus Whipple?'

'Miss Callender has just found a letter from him.'

'In the wastepaper basket?'

'No, actually in the library coal scuttle, oddly enough. I cannot imagine how it got there.'

'Sherlock Holmes used to keep his tobacco in the toe of a Persian slipper.'

'I don't think I have ever seen a Persian slipper.'

'Nor have I. It is my secret sorrow. Tell me about this letter from old Pop Whipple. Does he want an exclusive interview with the Empress?'

'He wants to come here and see her. He had heard so much about her, he says, and would like to take some photographs. He writes from the Athenaeum Club.'

'That morgue?' said Gally, who did not think highly of the Athenaeum. There was not a bishop or a Cabinet Minister there whom he would have taken to the old Pelican and introduced to Plug Basham and Buffy Struggles. He might be wronging the institution, but he doubted if it contained on its membership list a single sportsman capable of throwing soft-boiled eggs at an electric fan or smashing the piano on a Saturday night. 'I lunched with him there once.'

Lord Emsworth gasped, astounded.

'You mean you *know* Augustus Whipple?'

'Well, I've met him.'

'Why have you never told me?'

'I suppose the subject didn't come up. It was when I was thinking of writing my memoirs. I wanted some first-hand facts about an uncle of his who grew a second set of teeth in his eightieth year and used to crack Brazil nuts with them. Not at all a bad fellow. Whipple, I mean, not the uncle, who perished of a surfeit of Brazil nuts at the age of eighty-two. Are you going to have him to stay at the castle?'

'Of course. It will be a pleasure and a privilege.'

'The old shack's certainly filling up.'

'I have written a telegram explaining that I have only just seen his letter and inviting him to come here for as long as he wishes. I shall give it to Voules to send off. He is going to Market Blandings to take Egbert to his train.'

'Why don't you phone it?'

'I never seem able to make myself understood when I telephone the post office. There is an idiotic girl there who keeps saying "Pardon? Woodger mind repeating that?" No, I'll give it to Voules.'

'Give it to me. I'm going to the great city. There's a man there I want to see.'

'Why, thank you, Galahad. That will be capital.'

It was in mellow mood that Gally some minutes later set off down the drive, his hat jauntily on one side and his little legs twinkling. He was not actually singing a gipsy song as he trudged along, but it would have been unwise to have betted against his starting to do so at any moment, for this Whipple business had, he perceived, solved all the problems confronting him in his capacity of Sam's guardian angel. Reviewing the position of affairs, he summed it up as looking pretty smooth. He was well pleased with the way everything seemed to be turning out for the best.

The afternoon had now cooled off to some extent, but it was still warm enough to bring visions of the Emsworth Arms beer rising before the mental retina, and they rose before his. At the Emsworth Arms there was a large shady garden running down to the river, where you could sit and quaff beneath a spreading tree, your thirst agreeably stimulated by the spectacle of perspiring oarsmen toiling under the sun in boats often laden with a wife, two of her relations, three children, a dog and a picnic basket: and he was just thinking how extraordinarily well a foaming tankard would go down in these delightful surroundings, when he was aware of a voice saying 'Hoy!' and perceived a small boy at his side. The landlord of the Blue Boar's son Gary had proved faithful to his trust.

'Got a letter for you, Mr Threepwood,' he said. He had never met Gally socially, but like everyone else for miles around he knew him by sight.

Gally took the letter, mystified. The sepia maelstrom of the child's thumb had soiled it a good deal outwardly, but its contents were legible, and he found them disturbing. Sam had written briefly, confining himself to broad outlines rather than going into details, but he had made the main facts clear. He was not, it appeared, at the Emsworth Arms in Market Blandings but at the Blue Boar in Blandings Parva and for some reason he was in sore straits and would be glad of a word of advice from the addressee as to what to do for the best. Now, he implied though not actually saying so, was the time for all good men to come to the aid of the party.

No one had ever made a plea of this kind to Galahad Threepwood and found him unresponsive. The beer at the Blue Boar would, he knew, be vastly inferior to that of the Emsworth Arms, but he had always been a man able to take the rough with the smooth and he did not hesitate. A bare five minutes had elapsed before he crossed the Blue Boar's threshold.

3

In Sam's greeting there was a touch of the ship-wrecked mariner sighting a sail, for the interval between dispatching the note and seeing this friendly face had given him time for a further review of his situation. It had left him even more apprehensive than he had been at the beginning, and he had been distinctly apprehensive then. The day was warm, but his feet were cold. A bird twittering in the bushes outside sounded to his sensitive ear exactly like a police whistle.

Gally listened attentively as he poured out his tale. His manner, as it proceeded, gave no suggestion that he was shocked and horrified, nor was he. Of the broad general principle of hitting the police force in the eye he had always thoroughly approved. You could not, in his opinion, do it too much and too often. He could, however, see that his young friend had placed himself in a somewhat equivocal position. Steps would have to be taken through the proper channels if he was to be extricated from it, and fortunately he was able to take such steps.

'Tell me that bit about Sandy again,' he said. 'You say you saw her. Did she see you?'

'Yes.'

'And instantly, after one glance, streaked over the horizon?'

'Yes.'

'I don't like that.'

'I don't like it myself.'

'Not too promising, her attitude. It gives the impression that she didn't want to speak to you.'

'I thought of that, too.'

'This will have to be corrected. You then hared after her?'

'Yes.'

'With the watch in your pocket?'

'Yes.'

'The cop followed you and seemed anxious to effect a pinch?'

'Yes.'

'And you slugged him?'

'Yes.'

'Now I have it all straight. Your position, as I see it, is more or less that of the hart that pants for cooling streams when heated in the chase. You're a marked man. You can't go back to the Emsworth Arms.'

'I suppose not.'

'It isn't a question of supposing. Show your face there for a single instant and you haven't hope of escaping arrest. The arm of the law will grab you before you can say What-ho. You need a hide-out, and you will be glad to hear that I can provide one.'

Sam shook visibly.

'You can?'

'Most fortunately I am able to. For the next few days, till the hue and cry has died down, you must come and stay at the castle.'

'What!'

'You heard.'

'But didn't you tell me you weren't allowed to invite people to the castle?'

'I did. But it will be my brother Clarence who invites you, not I. He is at this very moment ordering the

96

vassals and serfs to get busy bringing the red carpet up
from the cellar and dusting it off in preparation for your
arrival. But I was forgetting that you are not abreast of
the latest developments. Let me briefly bring you up to
date. I happened to run into Clarence just now and found
him wreathed in smiles. His favourite reading, I must
mention, is a book on pigs by a fellow named Whipple.
He pores over it incessantly, savouring its golden words
like artichoke leaves. He is never happier than when
curled up with it. He must know it by heart, I should
think. All straight so far?'

'If you mean Do I follow you, yes. But I don't see –'

'Whither all this is tending? It won't be long before it
dawns on you. Shall I proceed?'

'Do.'

'Questioned, he revealed that young Sandy Callender
had found a letter from this Whipple asking if he can
drop in some time and have a look at Empress of
Blandings. You can readily imagine how it affected
Clarence. He started strewing roses from his hat and
dancing the Can-Can all over the premises. My cup
runneth over, he said, and he handed me a telegram to
send to Whipple urging him to pack a toothbrush and
come running. He gave him to understand that
Blandings Castle was his for as long as he cared to stay.
Now do you begin to get it?'

'No.'

'You don't see how this solves all your little
difficulties and makes your path straight?'

'No.'

'Not very quick at the uptake, are you? Your father
would have grasped it in a second. All you have to do is
present yourself at the front door and say "Yoo-hoo, I'm
Whipple" and you're in like Flynn, as the expression is.
After which, getting hold of young Sandy and making
her see the light will be a simple task. Extraordinarily
fortunate, Whipple having taken it into his head to write

to Clarence at just this time. Providential, I call it. One feels that one is somehow being *protected*.'

He had chosen a bad moment for placing his proposition before Sam, for the latter was in the very act of refreshing himself from his mug of beer. It was not until he had choked and gasped for a considerable space and been slapped a number of times on the back that he was able to speak. When he did, there was incredulity in his voice.

'You're crazy! What happens when Whipple turns up?'

'He won't.'

'Not when he gets that telegram?'

'He won't get it. What will reach him will be a regretful bob's-worth saying it's impossible to have him at the castle at the moment, as Clarence is in bed with German measles. I sent it off before I left.'

'Well, suppose there's somebody at the castle who knows me?'

'There isn't. You surely don't imagine I didn't think of that. You've never met my sister Hermione or her husband or Dame Daphne Winkworth, and you told me Tipton Plimsoll didn't know you by sight. Nothing to cause anxiety there.'

'How about Sandy?'

Gally was shocked.

'A nice girl like Sandy wouldn't dream of giving you away. I'm not saying she won't split a gusset when she finds how we have outmanoeuvred her, but her lips will be sealed. No, I can see no possible objection to what I suggest.'

'I can. I wouldn't do it for a thousand pounds. The mere thought of it makes my toes curl. I shall spend the night at this pub and after I've seen Sandy tomorrow I shall go back to London.'

Gally sighed.

'There's something wrong with the younger generation,' he said with a sad shake of the head. 'One

notices it on all sides. No dash, no enterprise, none of
the up-and-doing spirit. Any member of the old brigade
would have leaped to the task with his hair in a braid.
You won't reconsider?'

'No.'

'You would be under the same roof as the girl you
love.'

'For perhaps five minutes. At the end of that period I
can see the Lady somebody you spoke of, the one who
grabs people by their trouser seats, attaching herself to
mine and starting heaving. No, I am always willing to
oblige when feasible, but there are limits.'

'What if that copper finds you here and pinches you?'

'It would be unpleasant, I admit.'

'Well, then.'

'But I'd prefer it to going to Lord Emsworth and saying
"Yoo-hoo, I'm Whipple." '

Gally shrugged his shoulders resignedly, as Napoleon
might have done if he had asked his army to advance
and been told by them that they were not in the mood.

'Oh well,' he said, 'if you won't, you won't. But I still
consider your objections finicky. Then we'll just have to
carry on with the Visitors' Day programme.'

4

The car which was to take Colonel Wedge to Market
Blandings station and start him off on the first leg of his
journey into Worcestershire stood at the front door of
the castle with chauffeur Voules at the wheel. It was a
good car as cars went, but it paled into insignificance
beside the superlative Rolls which had been parked a
little farther along the drive. Colonel Wedge, coming out
of the house, eyed this ornate vehicle with respectful
admiration.

'Whose car is that, Voules?' he asked.

'Belongs to Mr Plimsoll, sir.'

Colonel Wedge could make nothing of this.

'To Mr *Plimsoll*?'

'Yes, sir. The gentleman arrived in it just now.'

The colonel continued bewildered. After what he had heard of the state of Tipton's finances, he would have expected him to arrive on roller skates. And it was as he stood blinking and trying to digest this piece of information that Tipton appeared in person, coming out of the house with an oblong object in his hand that seemed, as indeed it was, to be one of those cases in which jewellers put jewels.

'Oh, there you are, Colonel,' he said. 'I've been looking for you all over. Wanted to show you a necklace I picked up in London for Vee. I was hoping to give it to her directly I hit the joint, but darn it, they tell me she's not here. Great disappointment.' He opened the case. 'I think she'll like it, don't you?' he said, for he knew his loved one's fondness for bijouterie. Veronica Wedge was one of those girls who, if they have not plenty of precious stones on their persons, feel nude. Her aim in life was to look as like a chandelier as possible.

Colonel Wedge did not reply at once. A strange breathlessness had gripped him as he saw the contents of the case. He was no expert on jewellery, but if this necklace had not set its purchaser back what is technically known as a packet, he would be dashed.

'But –' he began, and paused, uncertain how to put it. You cannot ask your daughter's fiancé straight out how he is fixed as regards money in the bank. At least you can, but if you do, you risk the raised eyebrow and the frosty stare. 'But can you afford it, my dear fellow?' he asked, feeling that was a delicate way of approaching the subject.

Tipton was puzzled. He had been rich long enough for people to take his extravagances for granted.

'Why, sure,' he said. 'It only cost eight thousand pounds. They knocked off a bit for cash.'

It was established earlier in this narrative that Blandings Castle was a solidly constructed building, a massive pile with no tendency as a rule to wobble on its foundations, but to Colonel Wedge as he heard these words it seemed to be behaving like one of those Ouled Nail dancers he remembered having seen when a subaltern in Cairo. The same uninhibited twists and twiggles. Though not an unusually intelligent man, he was bright enough to gather that the Wedge family had done a remarkably foolish thing, in their haste depriving themselves of a son-in-law who drove around in five-thousand-guinea cars and thought nothing of paying eight thousand pounds for necklaces. They had, in short, goofed to precisely the same extent as the celebrated Indian who threw a pearl away richer than all his tribe. Veronica's letter breaking the engagement must even now be on its way to the castle, and the thought of what would happen when Tipton opened it and read the contents made Colonel Wedge look and feel as if he had received a crushing blow on the solar plexus.

'Not feeling well, Colonel?' asked Tipton, concerned.

'A touch of my old malaria,' the colonel managed to say.

'You get it often?'

'Fairly often. It comes on suddenly.'

'Too bad. Nasty thing to have.'

'Quite,' said Colonel Wedge, unaware that he was infringing Lord Emsworth's copyright material.

There remained one faint hope, that the letter, if written, had not yet been dispatched, and he was examining this hope and not thinking very highly of it, when Wilfred Allsop appeared at the head of the steps.

'Phone, Uncle Egbert,' he said. 'Aunt Hermione on the phone for you,' and few shots out of guns had ever travelled more briskly than did Colonel Wedge *en route* for the instrument.

'Hullo, old girl,' he panted, having reached and clutched the receiver.

'I am coming home the day after tomorrow, Egbert. You will have left for Worcestershire by then, I suppose.'

'I'm leaving this afternoon.'

'Don't stay there longer than you can help.'

'I won't. How about that letter?'

'Letter?'

'The one you were going to get Vee to write.'

'Oh, that? Have you been worrying about it? There was no need. You know what a sensible girl Veronica is. She quite saw that it was the only thing to do.'

'You mean she's written it?'

'Of course. I posted it just now. What did you say, Egbert?'

Colonel Wedge had not spoken. The sound to which she referred had been merely his hollow groan at the death bed of that hope. It had always been a sickly little thing, plainly not long for this world, and at these five words it had coughed quietly and expired.

'Nothing,' he said. 'Nothing. I am just clearing my throat.'

He debated within himself whether or not to break the bad news, and decided against it. Time enough for the old girl to learn the awful truth when she returned to the castle. Let her have one more day of happiness. 'Well, I suppose I'd better be getting along,' he said. 'Voules is waiting to take me to the train. When do you think that letter will get here?'

'Tomorrow morning, I imagine. Why?'

'I was just wondering.'

'Tipton will find it when he arrives.'

'He has arrived.'

'Oh, has he? Does he seem terribly depressed, poor fellow?'

A vision of Tipton gloating over that necklace, his

face split by an outsize in grins, rose before Colonel Wedge.

'No,' he said. 'No, not terribly.'

'How brave of him. I hope the letter will not upset him too much.'

'So do I,' said Colonel Wedge. 'So do I.'

A passer-by, seeing him as he came away from the telephone, would probably have supposed that the conversation just concluded had been one of no great importance, for there was nothing in his bearing to hint at the blow he had received. His backbone was rigid, his upper lip had not ceased to be stiff, nor did his moustache droop. Where Othello, with much less on his mind, had allowed his subdued eyes to drop tears as fast as the Arabian tree their med-cinable gum, he contrived to preserve an outward serenity. The British Army trains its sons well.

Nevertheless, his mind was in a whirl, the only thought in it that could possibly be called coherent being a wild regret that he had ever been misguided enough to believe in any statement made by his brother-in-law Clarence. Rashly he had forgotten the lesson that everyone who came in contact with the ninth Earl of Emsworth had to learn, that nothing he said was ever to be taken as making the remotest sense. The rule to live by was to ignore his every utterance.

He was still thinking bitterly about his relative by marriage as he came out of the front door. Tipton had disappeared, but his place had been taken by Gally. He was talking to Voules and seemed to be telling him a humorous story, for while the chauffeur was not actually smiling, chauffeurs not being permitted by their guild to do that, one noted a distinct twitching of the muscles around the lips.

'Ah, Egbert,' said Gally. 'You just off?'

At the sight of him something had seemed to explode

inside Colonel Wedge's head like a fire-cracker. It was an inspiration.

'Could I have a word with you, Galahad?' he said.

'Say on,' said Gally.

Colonel Wedge had no intention of saying on in the hearing of Voules, though he could see by the way the latter's ears were sticking up that he was perfectly willing to act as a confidant. He drew Gally aside to a spot where even the most clairaudient chauffeur, all eagerness to gather material for his memoirs, would be left out of the conversation. Privacy thus secured, he embarked on his narrative.

He told it well. At first perhaps there was a disposition on his part to diverge from the straight story line in order to insert acid criticism of Lord Emsworth, but he quickly overcame this tendency and placed the facts so clearly before Gally that the latter had no difficulty in grasping them and realizing the full gravity of the situation.

He felt that he did not need to look into a crystal ball to foresee what would happen when Tipton read that letter. His first move, one presumed, would be to ask Veronica for an explanation, and one could readily guess what explanation Veronica, the dumbest blonde in Shropshire and its adjoining counties, would give. 'But I thought you had lost all your money, Tip-pee,' she would say, rolling her lovely eyes, and it would be all over except for returning the presents, countermanding the bridesmaids, telling the caterer his services would not be required and breaking it to the bishop and assistant clergy that they would have to look for employment elsewhere. Those wedding bells, in short, would not ring out and Sam's sweepstake ticket would become a mere worthless scrap of paper, no good to man or beast. It would not be too much to say that Gally was appalled. In his consternation he even removed his

monocle and started to polish it, a thing he never did
except when greatly stirred.

'Egbert,' he said, 'that letter must not be allowed to
reach Tipton.'

'Exactly the idea that occurred to me,' said Colonel
Wedge. 'And what I was going to suggest was that you
should intercept it. You see,' he hastened to explain, 'I
can't do it myself, because I shan't be here. I've got to go
to my godmother's.'

'You can't give her a miss?'

'She would never forgive me.'

'Then, of course, my dear fellow, I shall be delighted
to place my services at your disposal.'

In the twenty-five years in which Colonel Egbert
Wedge had been married to Lord Emsworth's sister
Hermione quite a good deal of his wife's conversation
had dealt with the moral and spiritual defects of her
brother Galahad, but though he had prudently kept his
opinion to himself, she had never been able to shake
him in his view that Gally was the salt of the earth. He
had always been devoted to him and never more so than
at this moment.

'Good heavens, what a relief! You're sure you can
manage it?' he said, though he hardly knew why he had
bothered to ask the question. If good old Gally said he
would intercept a letter, that letter was as good as
intercepted. 'It'll mean getting up at some unearthly
hour.'

Gally waved his apologies aside.

'That's all right. If larks can do it, I can do it. So you
can go off and suck up to your godmother with a light
heart. And you ought to be starting, or you'll miss your
train.'

'I'm just waiting for that girl.'

'What girl?'

'That secretary of Clarence's. Her father has been

suddenly taken ill and she has to go away for a few days. Ah, here she is,' said Colonel Wedge as Sandy came down the steps. Her face was grave, as any girl's might be who was on her way to a parent's sick bed.

'I hope I have not kept you waiting, Colonel.'

'Not at all, not at all. Plenty of time.'

'I'm afraid I shall miss Visitors' Day, Gally.'

'Yes, I gathered that. I'm sorry to hear about your father.'

'Thank you, Gally. I knew you would be.'

'What's the matter with him?'

'The doctors are baffled. Hadn't we better be starting, Colonel?'

'Yes, carry on, Voules.'

The car drove off. Gally, a thoughtful frown on his face, continued to polish his monocle.

8

I

There is nothing that keys up the system like an eloquent pep talk, and Wilfred Allsop awoke next morning full of optimism and the will to win. 'My woman' he was murmuring as he shaved, 'My woman' he was saying to himself over the coffee and eggs at breakfast, and the words were still on his lips as he approached the Empress's sty some hour or two later with Tipton's flask in his pocket. Only when he reached his destination did there come to him the discouraging thought that things might not be going to go so neatly in accordance with plan as he had anticipated. The sty was there, the Empress was there, but of Monica Simmons there was no sign. He did not know what were the duties of a pig girl, but whatever they might be they had taken her elsewhere. To keep the record straight, one may mention that she was down at the pump in the kitchen garden, washing her face. A girl who is expecting an emotional scene with the man she loves naturally wishes to be at her best.

If there is one thing that damps a lover's spirit, it is the absence from the scene of action of the party of the second part who is so essential to a proposal of marriage, and this unforeseen stage wait had the worst effect on Wilfred's morale. The effervescent mood in which he had started out suffered a severe setback. He could feel his courage ebbing with every moment that passed. For the first time that day 'My woman' seemed to him a silly thing to say to anyone.

It was a moment for prompt action. He had taken one draught from the Tipton flask and had supposed that that would be sufficient but now he saw that the prudent course would be to take another. The old saying about spoiling ships for ha'porths of tar crossed his mind, together with the one that says that if a thing is worth doing, it is worth doing well. Convinced that he was on the right lines, he raised the flask to his lips, and he was leaning against the rail of the sty, his head tilted, when out of the corner of his eye he became conscious of a moving object not a dozen yards away and recognized it as Dame Daphne Winkworth's son Huxley, who, though Wilfred was not aware of it, had come to ascertain how chances were for letting the Empress out of her sty. He was a child with a one-track mind, and the desire to do this and see what happened had become something of an obsession with him.

To say that Wilfred was appalled would in no way be overstating the case. Huxley, he knew instinctively, was one of those boys who tell their mother everything. To be found fortifying himself from a flask by Huxley was precisely the same thing as being found by Dame Daphne in person. Quick thought was called for, and he thought quickly. Reaching behind him, he dropped the flask in the sty. It fell into the Empress's bran mash, which, he was relieved to see from a rapid glance, completely covered it. Feeling slightly restored, though still far from nonchalant, he turned to face the child, prepared to meet his charges, if any, with stout denial. All his life he had put great trust in stout denial, and it had always served him well.

Huxley, like Tipton, believed in getting down to brass tacks. He was not the boy to beat about bushes. He said, without preamble: 'I saw you drinking!'

'No, you didn't.'

'Yes, I did.'

'No, you didn't.'

'Yes, I did. Let me smell your breath.'

'I will not let you smell my breath.'

'Suspicious,' said Huxley. 'Highly suspicious.'

There was a pause, occupied by Wilfred in perspiring at every pore. Huxley resumed the conversational exchanges.

'Do you know what alcohol does to the common earthworm?'

'No, I don't. What does it do?'

'Plenty,' said Huxley darkly. He was silent for a moment, seeming to be musing on the tragic end of earthworms he had known. 'Mother says you're going to teach music at her school,' he resumed at length. 'Are you?'

'I am.'

'She won't like it if you spend your whole time drinking.'

'I do not spend my whole time drinking.'

'The hags aren't allowed to drink.'

'What do you mean, the hags?'

'The teachers. I call them the hags.'

'Try calling them the ladies of the staff.'

'Crumbs!' said Huxley, apparently not thinking well of the suggestion. He laughed an eldritch laugh. 'It's funny, isn't it?'

'What's funny?'

'You being a lady of the staff. Will they call you Ma'am?'

'Ah, shut up.'

'Or Miss?'

'I'm not keeping you, am I?'

Huxley said no, he was at a loose end. He returned to the aspect of the matter on which he had touched originally.

'Mother would sack you if she knew you were an alcoholic.'

'I am not an alcoholic.'

'She once sacked a hag for having a glass of sherry.'

'Very properly.'

'I shall have to tell her you were mopping it up.'

'I deny it categorically.'

'Let me smell your breath,' said Huxley, coming full circle, as it were.

Wilfred groaned in spirit. There was something about this child's conversational methods that gave him the illusion that he had fallen into the hands of the police. He did not know what future Dame Daphne Winkworth was planning for her son, but she would, he felt, be wise to have him study for the Bar. The boy seemed to him to possess all the qualities of a keen cross-examining counsel, the sort that traps a witness into damaging admissions and thunders an 'I suggest – ' or a 'Then am I to understand – ?' at him. And he was asking himself how long he would be able to hold his own in this battle of wills, when a hand reached past him and attached itself to the stripling's left ear, drawing from him an 'Ouch!' of anguish.

It was not merely the sight of Huxley in such close proximity to the Empress that had caused Monica, returning from her ablutions at the kitchen garden pump, to come galloping to the sty. She had also seen Wilfred Allsop, and the last thing she desired was to have a small boy a spectator of the tender scene which she hoped would shortly take place. If you have to have a small boy looking on when you have a tender scene, you might just as well not have a tender scene at all.

Accordingly, having grasped his ear and twisted it for the third time, she proceeded to lead Huxley across the meadow. She opened the gate at the end of it and pushed him through. Then, with a brief word to the effect that if she ever found him near the sty again she would strangle him with her bare hands, she came back to the man she loved.

Tumultuous emotions were stirring in Wilfred's bosom as he watched them go. Behind him he could hear the golloping sound of the Empress tucking into her bran mash, and at another and less tense moment he might have experienced some anxiety as to what the Scotch he had added to it would do to her if it acted so disastrously on earthworms. But now his thoughts were not on the Empress. There is a time for worrying about pigs and a time for not worrying about pigs.

His morale, lowered by those long minutes of waiting and further weakened by his chat with Huxley, had, he was glad to find, become completely restored. The few mouthfuls he had had time to imbibe from Tipton's flask had done their beneficent work. Once more he was feeling strong and masterful, and when she came back, he was ready for her. He strode up, he clasped her in his arms, he kissed her.

'My woman!' he bellowed in a tone somewhat reminiscent of a costermonger calling attention to his Brussels sprouts. Tipton had been perfectly right. It was, as he had said, as easy as falling off a log.

2

Visitors' Day at the castle always found Lord Emsworth ill at ease. It gave him the same apprehensive feeling as did the annual school treat, except that on Visitors' Day he did not have to wear a top hat. He was amiable and on the whole fond of his fellow men, but he preferred them when they remained aloof. It disturbed him when they came surging into his demesne, especially when their unions had been blessed and they brought their children with them. Children, unless closely watched, were apt to sneak off to the Empress's sty and do things calculated to wound that supreme pig's sensibilities. He would not readily forget the day when he had found her snapping feverishly at a potato on the end of a string, the vegetable constantly jerked from her lips by an uncouth little pip-squeak from Wolverhampton named Basil.

It was to prevent the repetition of any such horror that today, having seen the first char-a-banc arrive, he had set out for the sty armed to the teeth with a stout hunting crop, the blood of his Crusading ancestors hot within him. If Basil were paying a return date and had not undergone a spiritual change for the better since his last visit, he was in for an unpleasant surprise. By the time his host had finished with him he would know that he had been in a fight.

Avoiding the front door, for to go there would have meant passing through the hall where the personnel of the char-a-banc were keeping in line, not smoking and not fingering objects of art, he came out through a side entrance, and he had not gone far when his progress was arrested by Sam, who was trying to find the rendezvous which Gally had suggested. The three people he had so far asked to direct him to the Empress's sty had proved to be strangers in these parts themselves.

Sam, like Lord Emsworth, was not without his feeling of uneasiness on this Visitors' Day. The thought that Constable Evans, too, might have taken it into his head to have a look at the castle and its objects of art was not one that made for peace of mind. He had not liked meeting that zealous officer the first time, and something told him that it would be even more unpleasant meeting him again. It was difficult to shake off the feeling that he might appear at any moment round any corner, the handcuffs clinking in his pocket.

He also found Blandings Castle and its surroundings intimidating. To adjust himself to its impressive magnificence was not a simple task for one accustomed to the homelier atmosphere of Halsey Chambers, Halsey Court, London W1. Basil from Wolverhampton had taken the place in his stride, but it overawed Sam. It made him feel as if his hands and feet had swollen in a rather offensive manner and that his clothes had ceased to fit him.

This meeting with Lord Emsworth, accordingly, braced him like a tonic. His self-confidence functioned once more. If Blandings Castle could accept this seedy old man in his patched flannel trousers and battered fishing hat, he told himself, it could scarcely raise its eyebrows at one who in comparison was almost dapper.

'Good afternoon,' he said. 'I wonder if you could tell me how to get to the sty of the pig they call Empress of Blandings?'

Lord Emsworth's mild eyes glowed. It had always pained him when visitors on Visitors' Day trooped about the castle's interior goggling at pictures, tapestries, amber drawing-rooms and the like and never thought of going to see the one sight that mattered. He beamed at Sam, well pleased at having found a kindred spirit.

'I am going there myself,' he said, and his voice had a cordial ring. 'So you are a pig lover, too?'

Sam considered the question. He had never given much thought to pigs and, if asked, would probably have described himself as able to take them or leave them alone, but his companion had used the word 'too', seeming to indicate that these animals stood high in his estimation, so he felt it was only civil to reply in the affirmative. He did so, and was rewarded with a look of approval that convinced him that he had said the right thing.

'We go through the kitchen garden. It is the shortest way. Is this,' Lord Emsworth asked as they moved off, 'your first visit to Blandings?'

Sam said it was.

'Are you American?'

'No.'

'I thought you possibly might be. So many people are nowadays. I have just returned from America.'

'Oh yes?'

'I went to attend my sister's wedding. I stayed at an hotel in New York. Are you fond of boiled eggs?'

'Yes, I like boiled eggs.'

'So do I. But in America they serve them mashed up in a glass. It is one of the many curious aspects of the country. I objected strongly, but it did no good. Every time I asked for a boiled egg, up it came in a glass.'

'I suppose the solution would have been not to have asked for a boiled egg.'

'Exactly what my brother Galahad said. It would, he said, be the smart thing to do. But that's all very well, because suppose you want a boiled egg. It puts you in a bit of a fix.'

Sam was astounded. Unconsciously he had been picturing the proprietor of this super-stately home of England as a formidable figure on the lines of the old gentleman with the bushy eyebrows in *Little Lord Fauntleroy*, a book which twenty years ago he had read with considerable zest. The shock of finding that the patched and baggy object at his side owned the entire works was as great as that experienced by Colonel Wedge on the night when he had mistaken Lord Emsworth for the pigman's discarded overalls. It held him speechless until they had nearly reached the sty.

As they approached it, Lord Emsworth uttered an exclamation.

'Bless my soul, there's Wellbeloved.'

'I beg your pardon?'

'My former pigman,' said Lord Emsworth, indicating the figure slouched over the rail of the sty. 'He is in retirement now. I believe some relative of his left him a public house in Wolverhampton. He must have come in the char-a-banc from there. Ah, Wellbeloved,' he said. 'Come to have a look at the Empress?'

George Cyril Wellbeloved turned, revealing himself as a man with a squint and a broken nose, the former bestowed on him at birth, the latter acquired in the

course of a political discussion at the Goose and Gander
in Market Blandings in which he had espoused the
Communist cause.

'Hullo,' he said.

He spoke curtly. Between the manner of a pigman
dependent on his weekly wage and that of the owner of a
prosperous public house in Wolverhampton there is
always a subtle but well-marked difference. In George
Cyril's case it was more well-marked than subtle, for he
could not forget that twice during their mutual
association Lord Emsworth had dismissed him from his
service and dismissed him with contumely. These
things rankle. To be sacked once, yes, a man expected
that, it was part of the wholesome give and take
between employer and employed, but twice was a
calculated insult.

'Fat lot of having a look at the Empress I've been able
to do,' he said morosely. 'She's dug in in her shed and
won't come out,' he said, and Sam saw that at one end of
the sty there was a wooden shelter, presumably where
the silver medallist retired to sleep or to meditate.

'Strange,' said Lord Emsworth.

'Sinister, if you ask me. I'd say she was sickening for
something.'

'Nonsense. Try chirruping.'

'I have tried chirruping, and the more I chirrup, the
less she emerges. She's like the deaf adder in Holy
Scripture. I don't know if you're familiar with the deaf
adder. It comes in a bit in the Bible I used to learn at
Sunday School. Like the deaf adder it says, what don't
pay a ruddy bit of attention to the charmer, though he
charms till his eyes bubble. Try chirruping, indeed!' said
George Cyril disgustedly.

'You can't have chirruped properly. Chirrup again.'

'Not me, cocky, I've got a sore lip. You have a go.'

'I will.'

When it came to communicating with pigs, Lord

Emsworth had resources denied to other men. It so happened that there had come to Blandings Castle a year or so ago a young fellow anxious to marry one of his nieces, a young fellow who on leaving England under something of a cloud had found employment on a farm in Nebraska. He had forgotten his name, but he had never forgotten his teachings. In however deep a reverie a pig might be plunged, this young fellow had said, passing on the lore he had learned on the Nebraska farm, it could always be jerked out of it by what he described as the Master Call, and this he had taught to Lord Emsworth. It consisted of the word 'Pig-hoo-ey', the 'Hoo' to start in a low minor of two quarter notes in four-four time, building gradually from this to a higher note until at last the voice soared in full crescendo, reaching F-sharp on the natural scale and dwelling for two retarded half-notes, then breaking into a shower of accidental grace-notes.

It had taken Lord Emsworth some little time to master the technique, but he had succeeded eventually. So now, cupping his lips with both hands in order to increase the volume, he observed:

'Pig-Hoo-Ey!!!'

and Sam, who had not been expecting it, leaped like a lamb in springtime. The ejaculation seemed to him for a moment to have taken the top of his head off.

But he had not suffered in vain. Even before his ears had stopped ringing there came from the interior of the shelter a sound of stirring and rustling, as if a hippopotamus were levering itself up from its bed of reeds. Grunts became audible. The mild, kindly face of the Empress peered out, and a moment later it was possible to see her steadily and see her whole.

But not on Lord Emsworth's part with the pride and pleasure with which he was wont to see her. Something was plainly wrong with the silver medallist. She weaved, she tottered, she took a few uncertain steps towards the

trough, then slowly sank to the ground and lay there
inert.

'I told you so,' said George Cyril Wellbeloved. 'You
want to know what that is, chum?' he went on with
relish. 'That's swine fever.'

On Lord Emsworth the spectacle had had a paralysing
effect. If the phrase were not copyright, one might say
that his heart stood still. But his spirit remained
unimpaired. He glared militantly.

'Don't be a fool, Wellbeloved!'

George Cyril gave him a rebuking look.

'I suppose you know what happens when you call
your brother a fool,' he said austerely. 'You're in danger
of hell fire, that's what you're in danger of. You'll find it
in the Good Book. "If thou sayest to thy brother. Thou
fool . . ."'

'You're not my brother!' said Lord Emsworth, at the
same time thanking God.

George Cyril Wellbeloved would have none of this
quibbling.

'For purposes of argument I am. All men are brothers.
That's in the Good Book, too.'

'Get out! Get off my property immediately!'

'Okey-doke. George Cyril Wellbeloved does not
remain where he's not wanted, though it's a moot point
whether you're legally entitled to chuck the paying
public out on Visitors' Day. However, we'll waive that.
You'd better go and phone the vet,' said George Cyril
over his shoulder as he took a dignified departure. 'Not
that he'll be able to do a ruddy bit of good.'

Lord Emsworth was already on his way to telephone
the veterinary surgeon, his long legs flashing as he raced
to the house, and Sam, left alone, stood gazing at the
invalid. And as he gazed the sun came out from behind a
cloud and something glinted in the empty trough. It
looked like a flask. He climbed the rail and found that it
was a flask, and instantaneously all things were made

clear to him. He realized now why from the first the
Empress's aspect had struck him as vaguely familiar. He
had seen men come into the Drones Club smoking-room
on the morning after Boat Race night looking just like
that. Oofy Prosser practically always looked like that.
When Lord Emsworth returned, he was happy to be able
to calm his fears.

'It's all right,' he said.

'All *right*?' Lord Emsworth could not believe the ears
which exercise had reddened. 'If it's swine fever – '

'It isn't. Look at this.'

'What is that?'

'An empty flask. I found it in the trough.'

'God bless my soul, how did she get hold of it?'

'I wonder. But obviously all that's the matter is that
she's been on the toot of a lifetime. That pig is plastered.
You probably remember the old poem which begins
"The pig at eve had drunk its fill"?'

'No. No, I do not.'

'Well, that's what must have happened. She just needs
time to sleep it off. It's a pity we're so far from London.
There's a chemist in the Haymarket who fixes the most
wonderful pick-me-up. He could have put her right in no
time. Still, a good sleep will probably do the trick. You'll
see her turning cart-wheels tomorrow.'

Lord Emsworth drew a deep breath. He gazed at Sam
adoringly. He was not as a rule fond of his juniors, but
he could recognize merit when he saw it and it was plain
to him that here was something special in the way of
juniors, one whom he could take to his bosom and make
a friend of. And the thought that this young man, so
sound on pigs, so sympathetic in every way, would be
fading out of his life when Visitors' Day was over
horrified him. He wanted to see him constantly, to have
interminable talks on pigs with him, to wake up in the
morning with the heartening feeling that he would find
him at the breakfast table.

'Are you making a long stay in these parts?' he asked.

Sam, thinking of Constable Evans, said Well, that depended.

'You are not on a walking tour? Not got to get anywhere special?'

'No.'

'Then I wonder if you would care to be my guest at the castle for a few weeks? Or as long as you like, of course?'

If Sam had been able to speak, he would probably have said 'There *is* a Santa Claus! I do believe in fairies!' but this totally unexpected invitation had wiped speech from his lips. When he was able to utter, he said:

'It's awfully kind of you. I'd love it.'

'Capital! Capital, capital, capital!'

'Ah, there you are, my dear fellow,' said the cheery voice of Gally from behind them. 'So you've met Augustus Whipple, have you, Clarence?'

3

Lord Emsworth's pince-nez flew from their base. He shook from fishing hat to shoe sole. 'Whipple? Whipple? Whipple?' he gasped. 'Did you say Whipple?'

'Yes, this is Gus, as the boys at the Athenaeum call him. I suppose you weren't expecting him so soon. But that's what he's like. Never lets the grass grow under his feet and is always like lightning off the mark. Do it now is his slogan. Hullo, what's the matter with the Empress?'

'She is the worse for liquor, Galahad, I am sorry to say. Somebody carelessly dropped a flask of whisky in her bran mash.'

'What a lesson this is to all of us to keep off the sauce. We must try to get her to join Alcoholics Anonymous. Well, I'm glad there's no cause for alarm. A raw egg beaten up in Worcester sauce will probably work wonders. Still, I suppose you ought to have the vet take a look at her.'

'I have already telephoned him. He is on his way.'

'Then I'll take Whipple to your study and you can join us there after you've seen him.'

'Yes, yes, capital. This is a proud moment for me, Mr Whipple,' said Lord Emsworth, and Sam contrived to produce a weak smile. He was not yet equal to giving tongue, and he continued silent as Gally led him to the house. Fortunately Gally, as always, was able to provide conversation enough for two.

'Quick thinking, my boy, quick thinking,' he said complacently. 'I've always been a quick thinker. My resourcefulness was a matter of frequent comment at the old Pelican. "Galahad Threepwood," they used to say, "may not be much to look at, but you seldom find him at a loss." I remember once in those days glancing out of a window and seeing a bookie I owed money to at the front door. I saw that instant precautions would have to be taken, for my financial position was such that it would have inconvenienced me greatly to have been obliged to make a cash settlement at the moment. Only seconds elapsed before inspiration descended on me. When he hammered at my door, I was ready for him. "Have a care, Mr Simms," I shouted. He was Tim Simms, the Safe Man. "Keep away. I've got scarlet fever." He was incredulous, and said so. So I opened the door and he gave one look and was down the stairs in two strides. Most luckily one of my female acquaintances had happened to leave a lipstick in the sitting-room the day before, and I had been able to apply it to my cheeks. I caught a glimpse of myself in the mirror after he had left, and I can tell you it frightened *me*.'

'Listen,' said Sam.

'I know what you are going to say,' said Gally, checking him with a raised hand like a policeman directing traffic. 'You are all eagerness to ascertain why after your intransigent attitude of yesterday I decided to overrule your veto and tell Clarence you were Augustus Whipple. My dear boy, it was essential. You are not aware of it, but young Sandy with a snakiness which redounds little to her credit had slipped a fast one over on us. On some trivial pretext she had got leave from Clarence to go away for a day or two, thus rendering your prospects of a conference with her null and void. It became imperative, accordingly, to think up some way of introducing you into the house as a permanent guest, so that you would be on the spot when she came back, and this, as we have seen, I have been able to accomplish.'

'Listen,' said Sam, and again the raised hand checked him.

'I know you have some fanciful objection to being Augustus Whipple, but I think you will have to admit that the advantages outweigh the disadvantages. You're in the house, safe from Constable Evans, and when young Sandy returns, chuckling to herself as she thinks how she has outsmarted us, she will find you here and hit the ceiling. Weakened by the shock, she will be as dust beneath your chariot wheels. Yes, I think I am entitled to take a few bows for the way I have handled this rather delicate situation. There was talk at one time of my going into the diplomatic service, and I sometimes feel it was a pity I didn't. Well, here we are in Clarence's study. I must apologize for there being so little dust about. That's Sandy's fault. Take a seat and make yourself comfortable.'

Sam sat down and fixed him with an uncordial eye.

'Would you mind if I now slipped a word in edgeways?' he said coldly.

'Of course, my dear fellow. Go ahead. But I want no thanks.'

'Would it interest you to know that half a minute

before you came muscling in on us with your "Yoo-hoo, it's Whipple!" Lord Emsworth had invited me to stay at the castle for as long as I wanted to?'

It was not easy to dislodge the monocle from Gally's eye, but this piece of information did it. He stared incredulously.

'Are you pulling my leg?'

'I am not.'

'But what on earth made him do that?'

'He was grateful to me for assuring him that the Empress had not got swine fever.'

'And he really asked you to stay?'

'He did.'

Gally retrieved his monocle and replaced it in its niche. His manner was pensive.

'This opens up a new line of thought,' he said. 'It might perhaps have been better on the whole if I had not introduced the Whipple motif. It's a pity you didn't tell me that before.'

'When did I have a chance to?'

'True. Well, it's done now and nothing more to be said.'

'I can think of a few things.'

Gally looked pained.

'You must not allow yourself to become bitter, my boy. No doubt you are feeling disturbed and upset, but I can't see that you have much to complain of. You were in imminent danger of getting the local police force on the back of your neck, and the one thing you needed most sorely was a hide-out. Now you have one. What are those beautiful lines of someone's about the sailor being home from the sea and the hunter home from the hill? That's you. You're in, aren't you?'

'Under a false name.'

'What of that? There's nothing low or degrading about an alias. Look at Lord Bacon. Went about calling himself Shakespeare.'

'And I'm supposed to be an authority on pigs.'

'You have some objection to being an authority on pigs?'

'Yes, I have, considering that I don't know a dam thing about them except that their tails wiggle when they eat. What do I do when Lord Emsworth starts talking pig to me?'

'No need for concern. Clarence will do all the talking. An occasional low murmur is all he'll expect from you. But hist!'

'What do you mean, hist?'

'Seal your lips. I think I hear him coming.'

Gally was right. A moment later, Lord Emsworth bustled in, wreathed in smiles.

'Ah, here you are, Mr Whipple,' he said. 'Capital, capital. I will ring for tea.'

'Tea?' said Gally. 'You don't want tea. Filthy stuff. Look what it did to poor Buffy Struggles. Did I ever tell you about Buffy? Someone lured him into one of those temperance lectures illustrated with coloured slides and there was one showing the liver of the drinker of alcohol. He called on me next day, his face ashen. "Gally," he said, "what would you say the procedure was when a fellow wants to buy tea?" "Tea?" I said. "What do you want tea for?" "To drink," he said. I told him to pull himself together. "You're talking wildly," I said. "You can't drink tea. Have a drop of brandy." He shook his head. "No more alcohol for me," he said. "It makes your liver look like a Turner sunset." Well, I begged him with tears in my eyes not to do anything rash, but I couldn't move him. He ordered in ten pounds of the muck and was dead two weeks later. Got run over by a hansom cab in Piccadilly. Obviously if his system hadn't been weakened by tea, he'd have been able to dodge the vehicle. Summon Beach and tell him to bring a bottle of champagne. I can see from Whipple's face that he needs a bracer.'

'Perhaps you are right,' said Lord Emsworth.

'I know I'm right. The only safe way to get through life is to pickle your system thoroughly in alcohol. Look at Freddie Potts and his brother Eustace the time they ate the hedgehog.'

'Ate what?'

'The hedgehog. Freddie and Eustace were living on the Riviera at the time and they had a French chef, one of whose jobs was to go to market and buy supplies. On the way to Grasse that day, as he trotted off with the money in his pocket, he saw a dead hedgehog lying by the side of the road. Now this chef was a thrifty sort of chap and he saw immediately that if he refrained from buying the chicken he'd been sent to buy and stuck to the money, he'd be that much up, and he knew that with the aid of a few sauces he could pass that hedgehog off as chicken all right, so he picked it up and went home with it and served it up next day *en casserole*. Both brothers ate heartily, and here's the point of the story. Eustace, who was a teetotaller, nearly died, but Freddie, who had lived mostly on whisky since early boyhood, showed no ill effects whatsoever. I think there is a lesson in this for all of us, so press that bell, Clarence.'

Lord Emsworth pressed it, and Beach, resting in his pantry from the labours of the afternoon, was stirred to activity. Heaving himself up from his easy chair in a manner which would certainly have led Huxley Winkworth, had he seen him, to renew those offensive comparisons of his between him and Empress of Blandings rising from her couch, he put on the boots which for greater comfort he had removed and started laboriously up the stairs. His face as he went was careworn, his manner preoccupied.

In the nineteen years during which he had served Lord Emsworth in the capacity of major-domo it had always been with mixed feelings that Beach found himself regarding the weekly ceremony of Visitors' Day at Blandings Castle. It had its good points, and it had its drawbacks. On the one hand, it gratified his sense of importance to conduct a flock of human sheep about the premises and watch their awe-struck faces as he pointed out the various objects of interest: on the other all that walking up and down stairs and along corridors and in and out of rooms hurt his feet. It was a fact not generally known, for his stout boots hid their secret well, that he suffered from corns.

On the whole, however, the bright side may be said to have predominated over the dark side, the spiritual's pros to have outweighed the physical cons, and as a general rule he performed his task with a high heart and in an equable frame of mind. But not today. A butler who has been robbed of his silver watch can hardly be expected to be the same rollicking cicerone as a butler who has undergone no such deprivation. He had woken with his loss heavy on his mind, and as he led his mob of followers about the castle he was still brooding on it and blaming himself for not having kept a sharper eye on that fellow with whom he had collided in the entrance of the Emsworth Arms bar. He might have known that no good was to be expected from a man with a twisted ear.

On his departure for America to take up his duties in the offices of Donaldson's Dog Joy Inc. of Long Island City, the country's leading purveyors of biscuits to the American dog, Freddie Threepwood, Lord Emsworth's younger son, had bequeathed to Beach his collection of mystery thrillers, said to be the finest in Shropshire, and in three out of every ten of these the criminal, when unmasked, had proved to be a man with a twisted ear. It should have warned him, Beach felt, but unfortunately it had not, and it was with a feeling of dull depression that he entered the study.

The next moment, this dull depression had left him and he was tingling from head to foot as if electrified.

For there, apparently on the best of terms with his lordship and Mr Galahad, sat the miscreant in person. His head was bent as he scanned some photographs which Lord Emsworth was showing him, but that twisted ear was unmistakable.

It is probable that if Beach had not been a butler a startled cry would at this point have echoed through the room, but butlers do not utter startled cries. All he said was:

'You rang, m'lord?'

'Eh? Ah. Oh yes. Bring us a bottle of Bollinger, will you Beach.'

'Very good, m'lord.'

'And while it is coming, Mr Whipple,' said Lord Emsworth, 'there are some photographs of the Empress in the library I would like you to see.'

He led Sam from the room, and Gally was surprised to see that Beach, instead of following them, had remained behind and was approaching his chair in a conspiratorial manner. 'Could I have a word, Mr Galahad?'

'Certainly, Beach. Have several.'

'It is with reference to the gentleman,' said Beach, choking on the last word, 'who has just left us. Who is he, Mr Galahad?'

'That was my brother Clarence. You know him, don't you? I thought you'd met.'

Beach was in no mood for frivolity.

'The other gentleman, sir,' he said austerely.

'Oh the other one? That was Augustus Whipple, the author.'

The name was familiar to Beach. Lord Emsworth occasionally had trouble with his eyes and when so afflicted sometimes asked Beach to read him passages from *On The Care Of The Pig*, which Beach had always been happy to do, though no part of his duties. At the mention of it now he stared a pop-eyed stare.

'Whipple, Mr Galahad?'

'That's right. He wrote that pig book my brother's always reading. He's coming to stay here.'

'Sir!' said Beach, reeling.

Gally looked at him, surprised.

'What do you mean "Sir" and why does your jaw drop? Don't you like the idea?'

'No, Mr Galahad, I do not. The man is a criminal.'

'What on earth makes you think that?'

'He stole my watch yesterday at the Emsworth Arms, Mr Galahad.'

'Beach, I believe you've been having a couple.'

'No, sir. If I might tell you what transpired.'

Gally listened attentively to the twice-told tale. He thought Beach got even more drama out of it than Sam had done. When it was finished, he shook his head.

'Your story sounds very thin to me, Beach. On your own showing you only had a fleeting glance at the fellow.'

'Long enough to see his ear, Mr Galahad.'

'His what?'

'He had a twisted ear.'

Gally laughed indulgently.

'And you're making this extraordinary accusation purely because Whipple also had one? Good heavens, you can't go by that. Shropshire is stiff with men with twisted ears. I believe they form clubs and societies. Anything further?'

'Yes, sir, his age.'

'I don't get you.'

'He is not old enough to have written the book his lordship admires so much.'

'You find his appearance juvenile?'

'Yes, sir.'

'He tells me everybody does. He says it always surprises his fans to see how young he looks, but the explanation is very simple. For years he had been doing bending and stretching exercises every morning before breakfast. He also avoids all fried foods and never misses his Vitamins A, B and C twice a day. This keeps him fighting fit. He does seem young, I grant you that. But, dash it, Beach, you can't go about accusing respectable authors of nameless crimes just because their ears are a bit out of the straight and they aren't as elderly as you would like them to be. These cases of mistaken identity are very common. There was a man at the Pelican who was the living image of one of the Cabinet Ministers, which made it very awkward for the latter, as the Pelican chap was always getting thrown out of restaurants, frequently wearing a girl's hat. Didn't my nephew Freddie bequeath you all those mystery stories of his when he went to America?'

'Yes, sir.'

'You read them a good deal?'

'Yes, sir.'

'Well, there you are. They've inflamed your imagination and you see sinister characters everywhere. I believe Agatha Christie suffers in the same way. You mustn't let yourself get worried. Just accept the fact calmly that the bloke who was in here just now is Augustus Whipple all right and buzz off and get that Bollinger.'

Beach was so constructed that he could never be said actually to buzz off, his customary mode of progression being modelled on that of an elephant sauntering through an Indian jungle, but as he made his way to the cellar his pace was even slower than usual. A whirling mind often has this effect on the pedestrian, and his was whirling as it had seldom whirled before. He was convinced that the man to slake whose thirst he was fetching Bollinger was the man who had robbed him of his watch, but, if this was so, how had he come to be on such intimate terms with his lordship and Mr Galahad?

It was not an easy jigsaw puzzle to unravel, and he

delivered the refreshments to the study in a sort of
trance. He was still in the same condition when he
returned to the pantry and took his boots off again.
Shakespeare would have described him as perplexed in
the extreme. Erle Stanley Gardner would have drawn
inspiration from him for *The Case Of The Bewildered
Butler*. He himself, if questioned, would have said that
his head was swimming.

At times when the head swims, all butlers have the
means of restoring its equilibrium ready to hand. Port is
what works the magic. Beach kept a bottle in the pantry
cupboard, and he now reached for it. And he was about
to remove the cork, when the telephone rang.

He picked up the receiver and spoke in his usual
measured tones.

'Lord Emsworth's residence. His lordship's butler
speaking.'

The voice that replied was high and reedlike. Gally
would have called it the typical voice of a member of the
Athenaeum Club.

'Oh, good afternoon,' it said. 'This is Mr Augustus
Whipple.'

9

Visitors' Day had come and gone. The 'Kindly Keep in Line' and 'No Smoking' signs had been taken down, as had the one that urged the public not to finger objects of art. The char-a-bancs had left. George Cyril Wellbeloved had returned to Wolverhampton. Beach's feet had ceased to pain him. Except that the Empress had a severe hangover and was feeling cross and edgy and inclined to take offence at trifles, Blandings Castle might have been said to be back to normal.

At four o'clock or thereabouts on the following afternoon Lady Hermione Wedge alighted from the London train and stepped into the car which Voules the chauffeur had brought to Market Blandings station to meet her. Sandy Callender, who had travelled by the same train but in a humbler compartment at the other end of it, boarded the station taxi cab (Jno. Robinson, prop'r). And simultaneously Constable Evans of the local police force, mounting the bicycle which had now been restored to him, started to pedal castlewards to give Beach his watch.

The day seemed to be working up for a thunderstorm and her journey had left Lady Hermione a little tired, but relief made her forget fatigue. It was worth undergoing a certain amount of physical discomfort to feel that her child had been extricated from a most undesirable entanglement. Her thoughts, as Voules stepped on the gas, dwelt tenderly on Veronica, than whom no daughter could have been more cooperative, more alive to the fact that Mother knew best. Her attitude when taking down dictation from a parent's lips had been irreproachable. She could not have raised fewer objections if she had been a dictaphone. Once only had she spoken, and that was to ask how many s's there were in 'distressed'. 'Two, darling,' Lady Hermione had said, though actually there are three.

When you have a Voules at the wheel, it does not take long to get from Market Blandings station to Blandings Castle, and Lady Hermione found herself in her boudoir in good time for a cup of tea. She rang the bell, and Beach put on his boots, presented himself, booked the order and withdrew, to reappear after a brief interval accompanied by a footman bearing a laden tray. The footman – Stokes was his name, not that it matters – completed his share of the operations and melted away, and Lady Hermione, having poured herself a steaming cup and begun to sip, became aware that she still had Beach with her. He was standing in the middle of the room with something of the air of a public monument waiting to be unveiled, and his presence surprised her. It was not like him, when he had delivered the goods, to continue to hover around, and she bit into her cucumber sandwich with some annoyance, for she wished to be alone.

'Yes, Beach?' she said.

'Might I have a word, m'lady?'

Lady Hermione did not reply 'Have several' as Gally had done, contenting herself with inclining her head. She did this stiffly, her manner seeming to suggest that she was prepared to listen but that what he had to say had better be good.

The butler did not fail to sense this distaste for chit-chat.

'If you prefer it, m'lady, I could return later.'

'No, no, Beach. Is it something important?'

'Yes, m'lady. It is with reference to the gentleman who arrived yesterday as a guest at the castle,' said Beach, choking on the operative word as he had done in his interview with Gally.

Lady Hermione stiffened dangerously. An autocratic chatelaine, she resented guests arriving at the castle without her knowledge. She could scarcely believe that her brother Clarence would have had the temerity to invite a friend to stay unless he had first asked her permission, so she came – one might say leaped – to the conclusion that the mystery guest must be a crony of her brother Galahad, and her frown grew darker. One knew what Galahad's cronies were like. The dregs of civilization. A silver ring bookmaker was the least disreputable chum he would be likely to have added to the Blandings circle.

'Who is this man, Beach?' she demanded tensely.

'He gives his name as Augustus Whipple, m'lady.'

Lady Hermione's indignation subsided a good deal. Nobody could associate for long with Lord Emsworth without becoming familiar with the name Whipple, and she knew the author of *On The Care Of The Pig* to be a man of some standing in the best circles, a member of the Athenaeum Club, which she understood to be a most respectable institution, and an occasional adviser to the Minister of Agriculture. Clarence, she presumed, had invited him, and though she still felt that in doing so without consulting her he had been guilty of a solecism, she cooled off quite noticeably.

'Oh, Mr Whipple?' she said, relieved. The vision she had had of one of Gally's friends wearing a loud checked suit and addressing her as 'ducky' in a voice hoarsened by calling the odds at Sandown Park or Catterick Bridge faded. 'I shall be interested to meet him. Mr Whipple is a very well-known author.'

'If this *is* Mr Whipple, m'lady.'

'I don't understand you.'

'I suspect him of being an impostor,' hissed Beach. It is difficult, even if one wants to, to avoid hissing a sentence so well provided with sibilants, and he did not want to.

His statement ought not to have startled Lady Hermione as greatly as it did. She should have been used to impostors by this time. They had been in and out of Blandings Castle for years. A thoughtful writer had once said of the place that it had impostors the way other houses had mice. Nevertheless she uttered a sound which in a woman of less breeding might have been classified as a snort, and the buttered toast she was holding fell from her hand.

'An impostor!'

'Yes, m'lady.'

'But what grounds have you for saying such a thing?'

'It seemed to me peculiar that shortly after his arrival another gentleman should have rung up from London on the telephone saying that he, too, was Mr Augustus Whipple.'

'What!'

'Yes, m'lady. He was inquiring after his lordship's state of health. He informed me that he had received a telegram stating that his lordship was suffering from German measles. It renders one suspicious of the bona fides of the gentleman now in residence at the castle.'

'It certainly does!'

'I must confess to finding the whole situation mystifying.'

Lady Hermione was not mystified. Not, she might have said had she been capable of such vulgarity, by a jugful. As clearly as if the information had been written in letters of fire on the wall of the boudoir she saw behind this superfluity of Whipples the hand of her brother Galahad.

'Oh!' she said, and never had that monosyllable come closer to being the 'Ho!' of Constable Evans of the

Market Blandings police force. Her eyes were gleaming balefully. She looked like a cook who has encountered an intrusive black beetle in her kitchen. 'Will you find Mr Galahad and say I would like to see him. No, never mind, I will go and see him myself.'

2

Gally was in the billiards room when she found him, practising cannons with an expert hand. He laid down his cue courteously as she entered. He was not glad to see her, for it was his experience that her presence, like that of her sisters Constance, Dora and Julia, nearly always spelt trouble, but he did his best to infuse a brotherly warmth into his greeting.

'Hullo, Hermione. So you're back? Rotten day for travelling. You must have stifled in that train.'

There was nothing in Lady Hermione's manner to suggest that her feelings towards him were not friendly, or as friendly as they ever were. It was her intention to lull him into a false security before unmasking him and bathing him in confusion.

'It was rather stuffy,' she agreed. 'Do you think there's a storm coming up?'

'I shouldn't be surprised. How was Veronica?'

'She seemed very well.'

'I miss her bonny face.'

'I'll tell her. She'll be flattered. And how are *you*, Galahad?'

'Oh, ticking over much as usual.'

'And Clarence?'

'He's fine.'

Lady Hermione gave a little laugh.

'I'm talking as if I had been away a month. I suppose nothing has been happening since I left?'

'Nothing sensational. We have another guest.'

'Really? Who is that?'

'Fellow of the name of Whipple.'

'You don't mean Clarence's Whipple, the man who wrote that pig book he's always reading?'

'That's the chap. Clarence had a letter from him asking if he could come and take some photographs of the Empress, so of course he invited him to stay.'

'Of course. Clarence must be delighted.'

'Seventh heaven.'

'I don't wonder. There can't be many men like Mr Whipple.'

'Very few so pigminded.'

'I was not thinking of that so much as of his extraordinary gift for being in two places at the same time. I always think that makes a man so interesting.'

'Eh?'

'Well, you can't say it's not remarkable that he should be at Blandings Castle and still able to ring up on the telephone from London. I wonder how he does it. With mirrors, do you think?'

Gally was not easily disconcerted, and only the fact that he removed his monocle and began to polish it showed that her words had stirred him to any extent. Replacing the monocle, he said:

'Odd, that. Very curious.'

'So I thought when Beach told me. He took the call.'

'From Whipple?'

'Speaking from his London branch, not the Shropshire one.'

'He must have got the name wrong. One often catches names incorrectly on the telephone. What did this fellow say?'

'That he was Augustus Whipple and that he was calling to ask how Clarence was, as he had had a telegram saying that he was in bed with German measles. Quite a mystery, isn't it?'

Gally pondered for a moment. Then his face brightened.

'I think I see the solution. Simple when you give your mind to it. It was Visitors' Day yesterday and Beach had to work like a beaver all the afternoon showing the mob around the joint. He's not so young as he was and it took it out of him a lot. When it was over, he was at a low ebb and in need of a restorative. So what happens? He limps off to his pantry, reaches for the port bottle, incautiously overdoes it and becomes as soused as a herring, totally incapable of understanding a word said to him on the phone. The name he mistook for Whipple was probably Wilson or Wiggins or Williams, and what Wilson or Wiggins or Williams was saying was that *he* had got German measles. It's the only explanation.'

Many years previously in their mutual nursery Lady Hermione, even then a force to be reckoned with, had once struck her brother Galahad on the head with her favourite doll Belinda, laying him out as flat as a Dover sole. She was wishing she could put her hands on a doll now. Or she would have been prepared to settle for a hatchet.

'I can think of another,' she said, 'and that is that for some reason at which I cannot attempt to guess you have sneaked one of your impossible friends into the castle. I should say one more of your impossible friends, because this is not the first time it has happened. Who is this man?'

'You want me to come clean?'

'If you will be so good.'

'He's a chap called Sam Bagshott.'

'Wanted by the police, no doubt?'

'Oddly enough, yes,' said Gally with a touch of admiration in his voice. This exhibition of woman's intuition had impressed him. 'But that was due to an absurd misunderstanding. He's a most respectable fellow really. Son of my old pal Boko Bagshott. And he's here because he's jolly well got to be here. It's imperative that he confers with the Callender girl, whom he loves but by whom he has been given the air, and she's away and nobody knows when she'll be back. Obviously he must stay put and await her arrival.'

'Oh, must he? I disagree with you. If you think he is going to remain here another day, you are very much mistaken. I shall tell Beach to see that his things are packed and that he is out of the place in the next half-hour.'

Gally continued tranquil.

'I wouldn't.'

'And if I were not a very tolerant and easygoing woman, he would not be given time to pack.'

'I still maintain that you would be making a mistake.'

'I suppose that remark has some sort of meaning, but I cannot imagine what.'

'It will flash on you in a moment. I must begin by mentioning that I had a chat with Egbert before he left.'

'Well?'

'He said you had gone to London to get Veronica to write to Tipton breaking the engagement.'

'Well?'

'It bewildered me. I should have thought an up-and-coming young multi-millionaire would have been the son-in-law of your dreams. Aren't you fond of multi-millionaires?'

'Tipton is not a multi-millionaire. He has lost all his money speculating on the Stock Exchange.'

'You astound me. Who told you that?'

'Clarence.'

'And you really look on Clarence as a reliable source?'

'In the present case, yes. He had the information from Tipton himself.'

'It didn't occur to you that Clarence, acting true to the form of a lifetime, might have got everything muddled up? Let me brief you as to the real position of affairs. Tipton hasn't lost a penny, but like many a better man before him he was in chokey and needed bail. He hadn't the price on him, somebody in the course of the evening having pinched his wallet, so he rang Clarence up at his hotel, said he had lost all his money and could Clarence oblige him with a loan of twenty dollars. That's the whole story. If you have any lingering doubt in your mind as to Tipton's solvency, let me tell you that when he blew in the day before yesterday he was at the wheel of a Rolls Royce and waving an eight-thousand-pound necklace, a little gift for Vee which he had picked up in London. I was not privileged to see his underclothing, but I should imagine it consisted of thousand dollar bills. Fellows like Tipton always wear them next the skin.'

Some people on receiving a shock turn pale, others purple. Lady Hermione did both. The colour faded from her cheeks, then rushed back. There was a settee near where she stood. She sank on to it bonelessly, staring as if she were seeing some horrible sight – some sight, that is to say, even more horrible than a brother with a black-rimmed monocle in his right eye. Her breath came in short gasps, and Gally hastened to supply aid and comfort. He was a humane man and had no wish to see a blood relation keeling over in an apoplectic fit.

'It's all right,' he said. 'You can stop swooning. Egbert asked me to intercept Veronica's letter before it could reach Tipton, so I got up at the crack of dawn and did.'

The relief that flooded over Lady Hermione was so stupendous that she could not speak. The whole world, even Gally, seemed beautiful to her. Having gurgled for a while, she said:

'Oh, Galahad!'

'I thought you'd be pleased.'

'Where is it? Give it to me.'

'I haven't got it.'

Lady Hermione, who had been lying back, sat up with a jerk.

'You've lost it?' she cried, the apoplectic fit threatening to return.

'No, I've not lost it. I've given it to Sam. Whether or not he hands it on to Tipton depends on you. Accept him as an honoured guest and give him that sunny smile of yours from time to time, and you'll be as right as rain. But the slightest relaxation of old-world hospitality on your part and Tipton's mail will be augmented by a communication from the girl he loves. You had better begin practising being the ideal hostess without delay, for both Sam and I have high standards and you mustn't fall short of them,' said Gally, and feeling that this was about as telling an exit line as could be found on the spur of the moment he replaced his cue in the rack and left the room.

It was only when he reached the smoking-room which was his objective and saw Sam sitting there, on his face the dazed look of one who has recently concluded a long conversation on pigs with Lord Emsworth, that a sudden thought struck him. His sister Hermione was a woman for whom as an antagonist he had a great respect, and he knew that she was not one meekly to accept defeat. She might be down, but she was never out. It was highly probable that Sam, all unused as he was to the methods of jungle warfare prevailing in Blandings Castle and little thinking that that was the first place his hostess would search, would have put that letter somewhere in his bedroom. Precautions, he saw, must be taken immediately, for he knew the search would not be long delayed.

'Sam,' he said, 'what did you do with that letter I gave you?'

'It's in my room.'

'As I thought. Just as I had suspected. Go and get it.'

'Why?'

'Never mind why. I want it, and let us hope it's still

there. Ah,' he said, when Sam returned, 'all is well. Prompt action has saved the day. Give it to me.'

'What are you going to do with it?'

'I am going to enclose it in a stout manila envelope and tuck it away in a drawer of Clarence's desk. Even Hermione,' said Gally with pardonable complacency, 'won't think of looking there.'

3

In predicting that Lady Hermione would shortly be instituting a search of Sam's room Gally had not erred. Even as he was speaking she had registered a resolve to explore its every nook and cranny. Her first move after Gally had left her had been to telephone her daughter Veronica and explain the facts relating to Tipton's financial status, and when Veronica had uttered a squeal similar in volume to that of George Cyril Wellbeloved's niece Marlene and stammered, 'But, Mum-mee, what about my letter?' she had assured her that she must not feel uneasy about that because Mother had everything under control and Tipton would never see it. She then set out in quest of her nephew Wilfred Allsop, whom she proposed to enrol as an assistant in her investigations. She found him in the hall, meditatively tapping the barometer that hung there, and brusquely commanded him to stop tapping and accompany her to her boudoir.

Except for observing that according to the barometer, which had been very frank on the point, there was going to be the dickens of a thunderstorm any minute now, Wilfred had nothing to say as they went up the stairs. From childhood days the society of his Aunt Hermione had always occasioned him the gravest discomfort, making him speculate as to which of his sins of commission or omission she was about to drag into the light of day and comment on in that forthright manner of hers. Even though his conscience at the moment was reasonably clear, he could not help a twinge of apprehension as they reached the boudoir and she curtly bade him take a seat. He did not like her looks. It was plain to him that she was on the boil. If ever he had seen a fermenting aunt, this fermenting aunt was that fermenting aunt.

To his relief he found that it was not he who had caused her blood pressure to rise. When she spoke, she was, as aunts go, quite civil, not actually cooing to him like a turtle dove accosting its loved one but with nothing in her manner reminiscent of the bucko mate of an old-fashioned hell ship addressing an able-bodied seaman whose activities had dissatisfied him.

'Wilfred,' she said, 'I want your help.'

'My what?' said Wilfred, amazed. He could imagine no situation to which this masterful woman would not be equal without outside support. Unless, of course, she was doing a crossword puzzle and had got stumped by a word of three letters beginning with E and meaning large Australian bird, in which event his brain was at her disposal.

'You must treat what I say as absolutely confidential.'

'Oh rather. Not a word to a soul. But what's all this about?'

'If you will be good enough to listen, I will tell you. A serious situation has arisen. Have you met this Augustus Whipple who came here yesterday?'

'Seen him at meals. Why?'

'He is not Augustus Whipple.'

'The story that's going the rounds is that he is. Uncle Clarence keeps calling him Mr Whipple.'

'I dare say, but he is an impostor.'

'Good Lord! Are you sure?'

'Quite sure.'

'Then why don't you boot him out?'

'That is what I am about to tell you. I am helpless. He has got a letter from Veronica.'

'She knows him?'

'Of course she does not.'

'Then why the correspondence?'

'Oh, Wilfred!'

'It's all very well to say "Oh, Wilfred!" in that soupy tone of voice, but you're making my head go round. If Vee doesn't know him, how do they come to be pen pals? I don't get it.'

'The letter was written to Tipton.'

'To Tippy?'

'Yes.'

'Let's get this straight. You say the letter was written to *Tippy*?'

'Yes, yes, YES!'

With a wide despairing gesture Wilfred knocked over a small table containing a vase of roses and a photograph of Colonel Wedge in the uniform of the Shropshire Light Infantry.

'Well, if you think that makes it all clear, you're very much in error. I fail absolutely to understand where Tippy comes into the thing. I simply can't see –'

'Wilfred!'

'Hullo?'

'Stop *talking*! How can I explain if you persist in interrupting me?'

'Sorry. Carry on. You have the floor. But I still say you're making my head go round.'

'It is all quite simple.'

'Says you!'

'What?'

'I didn't speak.'

'You said something.'

'Just a hiccup.'

'Oh? Well, as I said, the whole thing is quite simple. Veronica happened to be feeling depressed and nervous for some reason, and in this mood of depression she felt that she was making a mistake in marrying Tipton. So she wrote him a letter breaking off the engagement. She now of course bitterly regrets it, but the letter was posted.'

'When?'

'Two days ago.'

'Then Tippy must have had it by now.'

'I keep telling you this man has got it. He intercepted it and is – '

'Holding you up?'

'Exactly.'

'What does he want? Money?'

'No, not money. But he will give the letter to Tipton if I do not allow him to stay on at the castle.'

'And you don't want him?'

'Of course I do not want him.'

'Well,' said Wilfred, breaking the bad news, 'it looks to me from where I sit as if you'd jolly well got him. He has you by the short hairs. You can't afford to let Tippy see that letter. Once let his eye rest on it and bim go your hopes and dreams of a millionaire son-in-law.'

An uneasy silence followed. It was broken by Wilfred saying that in his opinion his cousin Veronica ought to lose no time in putting in an application for a padded cell in some not too choosy lunatic asylum. The remark roused all the mother in Lady Hermione.

'What do you mean?' she demanded hotly.

'Writing a letter like that! She must have been cuckoo.'

'I told you she was depressed.'

'Not half as depressed as she'll be when Tippy walks out on her. I repeat that she ought to have her head examined.'

Lady Hermione was finding her nephew's manner, so different from his customary obsequiousness, extremely trying, but this was no time for rebuking him. It seemed

to her that if these slurs on her daughter's intelligence
were to be rebutted, it would be necessary to reveal the
true facts. Reluctantly she did so.

'Veronica is not to be blamed. I was under the
impression, misled by your Uncle Clarence, that Tipton
had lost all his money. I naturally could not allow her to
marry a pauper. One has to be practical. So I advised her
to break off the engagement.'

'Oh, I see. Didn't she object?'

'She seemed a little upset at first.'

'I'm not surprised. She's nuts about Tippy.'

'But she is a sensible girl and saw how out of the
question the marriage would be.'

'It'll be out of the question all right if Tippy sees that
letter.'

'He will not see it. I am going to search this man's
room and find it and destroy it.'

Wilfred goggled. Years of association with her had left
him with no doubt as to his Aunt Hermione being a
pretty hard-boiled egg, but he had never suspected her to
quite such twenty-minutes-in-the-saucepan-ness as this.
He had always supposed that her hardboiled eggery
expressed itself in words not deeds. A gurgling sound
like the wind going out of the children's toy known as
the dying duck showed how deeply he had been moved.

'Search his room?'

'Yes, and I want you with me.'

'Who, me? Why me?'

'I shall need you to stand outside the room and give
me warning if you see anyone coming. I think you had
better sing.'

'Sing?'

'Yes.'

'*Sing?*'

'Yes.'

'Sing what?'

Lady Hermione had often heard of secret societies

where plotters plotted plots together, but she wondered if any plotter in any secret society had ever had so much difficulty as she was having in driving into the head of another plotter what he the first plotter, was trying to plot. It was with an effort that she restrained herself from uttering words which would have relieved her but must inevitably have alienated the only possible ally on whose services she could call. She contented herself with a wide despairing gesture similar to her nephew's.

'What does it matter what you sing? I am not asking you to appear on the concert platform. You will not be performing at Covent Garden. Sing anything.'

Wilfred mentally ran through his repertoire and decided on that thing about having another cup of coffee and another piece of pie which Tipton had taught him in the course of their revels in New York. He liked both words and music, the work, he had been given to understand, of the maestro Berlin, author and composer of *Alexander's Ragtime Band* and other morceaux.

'Well, all right,' he said, though not with any great enthusiasm. 'And what will you do then?'

'I shall make my escape.'

'Down the water pipe?'

'Through the french window and out on to the lawn. The man has been given the Garden Suite,' said Lady Hermione bitterly. She would have resented an impostor being housed even in a garret and the Garden Suite was the choicest locality that Blandings Castle had to offer. It was where you put guests like the Duke of Dunstable, for whom the best was none too good.

His aunt's statement that he was to play a prominent part in this cloak-and-dagger enterprise had caused Wilfred Allsop to look like a nephew on whose head the ceiling has unexpectedly fallen, and that is how he was looking as she proceeded.

'The first thing to do is to get the man out of the way.'

'What!'

'Go and tell him that your Uncle Clarence is waiting
to see him at the Empress's sty.'

'A very sound idea,' said Wilfred, much relieved. Her
use of the expression 'get out of the way' had misled him
for a moment. He had feared that she was going to
suggest that he waylay this synthetic Whipple and set
about him with a meat axe. He would not have put it
past her. The lengths to which she appeared prepared to
go seemed to him infinite, and he had been feeling like
Macbeth talking things over with Lady Macbeth. It was
with a heart lighter than he had supposed it would ever
be again that he rose and set off in quest of Sam.

Sam was still in the smoking-room when Wilfred
found him, and he received his message without
pleasure. In the short time in which he had known him
he had conceived a great liking for Lord Emsworth and
would have been glad whenever the latter wished to chat
with him about the Brontë country or the Land of
Dickens or indeed about anything except pigs, but
something told him that it would be upon these
attractive animals that his host would touch when they
met. However, it being impossible to ignore the
summons, he started out for the sty, taking the short cut
through the kitchen garden which they had taken on the
previous day, and Constable Evans, standing at the
window of Beach's pantry with a glass of port in his
hand, had an excellent view of him as he passed. For an
instant he stood staring, then with a brief 'Ho' he laid
down his glass and sallied out in pursuit. No leopard on
the trail could have flung itself into the chase with
greater abandon. It was his first chance in months of
making a pinch that amounted to anything and he was
resolved to seize it.

The first thing Sam noticed on arriving at the sty was
a complete shortage of Lord Emsworths and he could
make nothing of it, for Wilfred had distinctly told him
that his host was awaiting him there. Some mistake, he

assumed, and glad of the respite he lit a cigarette. And he had scarcely done so when there was a flash and a roar and the storm which had been threatening all the afternoon broke with a violence which probably came as a surprise to the barometer Wilfred had tapped in the hall. It had predicted dirty weather, but it could hardly have anticipated anything on this scale. To Sam, whose nervous system was not at its best, what was in progress seemed to combine the outstanding qualities of the Johnstown flood and the Day of Judgement.

It was a moment to seek shelter, and most fortunately there was shelter within easy reach. At the junction between the kitchen garden and the meadow where the Empress had her headquarters there stood what looked like – and indeed was – a potting shed. Its interior, he presumed, would be stuffy and probably smelly, but these disadvantages were outweighed by the fact that it would be dry, and dryness was what he wanted – or, as he would have said when writing a review for one of the higher-browed weeklies, desiderated. He was inside it in a matter of seconds and was congratulating himself on the promptness with which he had acted, when the door slammed behind him and he heard the shooting of a bolt. It surprised and disconcerted him.

'Hoy!' he cried, and from outside a voice spoke, the cold, metallic voice of a policeman who has effected a fair cop.

'You're pinched,' it said.

Silence followed. It had been Constable Evans's original intention on seeing Sam enter the shed to go in after him and take him into immediate custody, but second thoughts had led to a change of plan. Better, he felt, to wait till he could bring up reinforcements. He could not forget that this particular malefactor packed a wicked wallop, and he had no desire to be on the receiving end of it again. So having shot the bolt and said, 'You're pinched' he hastened back to Beach's pantry to telephone the police station to send a car and an assistant, preferably a large and muscular one.

It was some light consolation to Sam to feel that he must be getting soaked to his underlinen.

10

I

It was the boast of Jno. Robinson, its proprietor, that the station taxi, though a little creaky in the joints and inclined to pant when going uphill, never failed to get its patrons to their destination sooner or later, and it had got Sandy to hers without mishap. Her first move on arrival, like a conscientious secretary, was to go and report to Lord Emsworth, whose jaw dropped slightly when he saw her, for he had been hoping that she would have been away rather longer. She then went to the small room opening off the library where she worked.

She was not long without company. Musing on life in a deck chair on the front lawn, Gally had seen her drive up, and though reluctant to stir from his comfortable seat he felt it imperative to seek her out and put her in touch with recent developments at the castle. He also proposed to chide her for sneaking off as she had done. She had behaved, he considered with a low cunning which he deplored. He had always been a man who disliked having a fast one put over on him, and he was prepared to be somewhat stern with Sandy.

Sandy, for her part, was prepared to be somewhat stern with him. On seeing Sam emerge from the Emsworth Arms bar she had been sure that Gally was responsible for his being there, and it was at him even more than at Sam that her resentment was directed. Their meeting, consequently, was marked by a certain frostiness on both sides. She greeted him with a cold 'Good evening', and he said, 'Take that lemon out of your mouth, Mona Lisa. I want a word with you.'

Sandy continued haughty. Her full height was not much, but she drew herself to what there was of it.

'If it's about Sam – '

'Of course it's about Sam.'

'Then I don't want to hear it.'

A less courageous man than Gally might have quailed at the iciness of her tone, but it left him undaunted.

'What you want and what you're going to get,' he said, 'are two substantially different things. Sam has told me all about that Drones Club sweepstake and the offer from the syndicate and how you tried to get him to sell out for a hundred pounds when he had only to sit tight and let nature take its course in order to clean up on a really impressive scale, and frankly I was appalled. Your mutton-headedness stunned me.'

'I don't consider that I was mutton-headed, as you call it.'

'Then your standards must be very high.'

'I had a good reason for wanting him to sell out. I knew what Tipton was like.'

'He's rather like a string bean, but I don't see how that enters into it.'

'I'm not talking about what he looks like. The sort of man he is, I mean.'

'And what sort is that?'

'Susceptible. Always falling in and out of love. When I was working for his uncle, he got engaged to a whole series of girls, and every time the engagement was broken off. I supposed that this latest one would follow the usual pattern.'

'Often a bridesmaid but never a bride, you felt? You were mistaken. His passion for Veronica is the real thing. When he fetched up here the day before yesterday, it was with the love light in his eyes and an eight-thousand-pound necklace for her in his trouser pocket. He'll be a married man in next to no time. The date is set, the caterer notified, the bishop and assistant clergy lined up at the starting gate waiting for the flag to fall.'

'And suppose she breaks off the engagement? Tipton's girls always do.'

'Not this one. Sam's on a certainty. If ever there was a Today's Safety Bet, this is it. My advice to you, young Sandy, is to admit you were wrong and kiss and make up. When you see him –'

'I shan't see him.'

'Oh yes, you will. He's here now.'

'I know he is. At the Emsworth Arms.'

'Not at the Emsworth Arms, at the castle.'

'What!'

'Passing for the moment under the name of Augustus Whipple.'

'What!'

'You do keep saying "What", don't you? Yes, on my advice he assumed the name of Whipple, for I felt it would endear him to Clarence, as indeed it has. And that brings me to another talking point. If ever you entertained doubts as to the wholeheartedness of his love, reflect that simply in order to be near you and plead his cause he has placed himself in a position where he has to listen to Clarence talking pig to him from morning to night. He's suffering agonies, and all for you. So be guided by me, young Sandy, and fling yourself into his arms and murmur "Oh, Sam, can you ever forgive me?" or "Oh, Sam, let the past be forgotten" or, of course,' said Gally, always ready to make concessions, 'any other gag along those lines you may prefer. I'll leave you to think it over.'

His story had shaken Sandy. It had been well said of Galahad Threepwood in his Pelican Club days that few could equal him at telling the tale. He was credited by his associates with the ability to talk the hind leg off a donkey, and the passage of the years had in no way diminished his spellbinding qualities. Half an hour ago the idea of ever speaking to Sam again in this world or the next would have seemed to Sandy so bizarre as not to deserve consideration, but now she was beginning to feel that that idea of flinging herself into his arms might have something in it.

Like so many girls with similarly coloured hair, she had a low boiling point and was easily stirred to sudden furies, but they resembled those of the storm outside, which after a sensational start had already begun to calm down, in being soon over. Looking out of the window, she saw that the Niagara of a few minutes back was now a gentle trickle and the thunder and lightning had ceased altogether. It was as if the forces of Nature felt that they had made their point and could relax, and she found herself in harmony with their softened mood.

Ever since the morning when Sam had spoken his mind to her on the subject of ginger-haired little fatheads and she had thrown the ring at him she had tried to keep resentment alive, but she had never really liked the idea of not speaking to him again in this world or the next. She had told herself that he was the obstinate pig-headed type whom no girl of sense would dream of marrying and that the severance of relations between them was the best thing that could have happened, but all the while a voice within her had kept reminding her that, even though pig-headed, he was unquestionably a lamb, and lambs are not so easily come by in these hard times that you can afford to throw them carelessly away. Remorse, in short, had gnawed her, causing her to feel almost precisely as Colonel Wedge and his wife Hermione had felt on discovering that they had rashly given the bum's rush to a prospective son-in-law who oozed dollar bills at every pore.

On only one point had Gally left her dubious, and that was the likelihood of Tipton Plimsoll becoming a

married man. She had seen so many of his false starts
when she had been working for his Uncle Chet that she
could not believe that any betrothal of his could possibly
culminate in a wedding. Recalling his long line of
fiancées, all of whom had come and gone with a
quickness that deceived the eye, she was unable to
picture him lined up with this latest one at the altar
rails. It would be necessary, therefore, even while
flinging herself into Sam's arms, to make it quite clear
to him that her views on the syndicate's offer had in no
way changed. On this she was resolved to be firm. Lamb
or no lamb, he would have to accept her ruling.

She had reached this point in her meditations, when
something long and string-bean-like bounded in with a
'Hi!' that rattled the window pane and for the first time
since she had left her native America she beheld Tipton
Plimsoll.

Her presence at the castle had astounded Tipton.
Looking out of the smoking-room window, he had seen
the station taxi drive up and a girl whom his experienced
eye classified as quite a dish alight from it. Her
appearance had seemed to him oddly familiar, but it was
only when she raised her head while handing Jno.
Robinson his fare that he recognized her as one of his
closest and most esteemed buddies.

He was exuberantly glad to see her. He had always
been devoted to Sandy. Her place in his life had been
that of a kindly sister in whom he could confide
whenever he fell in love with someone new and needed
the services of a confidant. She had given him
encouragement when he required it and sympathy when
he required that, which usually happened a few weeks
after he had become engaged, for his fiancées had a
disconcerting knack of writing to tell him they were
sorry but they had just married elsewhere, adding in a
postscript that they would always look on him as a dear
friend.

'Sandy Callender as I live and breathe!' he cried. 'I couldn't believe it when I saw you getting out of that cab. I didn't even know you were on this side. What on earth are you doing here?'

'I'm Lord Emsworth's secretary. Gally Threepwood got me the job. I met him in London just when his sister was looking around for someone to work for Lord Emsworth. Well, it's wonderful seeing you again, Tipton. How are you?'

'Pretty spruce, thanks.'

'That's good. I hear you're engaged again.'

Tipton lost some of his joyous effervescence. Not meaning to wound, she had said the wrong thing.

'Don't say "again",' he protested, 'as if it was something I did every hour on the hour.'

'Well, isn't it?'

Tipton was forced to concede that there was a certain amount of justice in the question.

'Well, yes,' he admitted, 'I have got tangled up with a girl or two –'

'Or three or four or five.'

' – in my time, but that was just kid stuff. This is the real thing. This is for keeps. You remember those other babes I got starry-eyed about?'

'Doris Jimpson, Angela Thurloe, Vanessa Wainwright, Barbara Bessemer . . .'

'All right, all right. No need to call the score. What I was going to say was Do you know what was wrong with them?'

'They married somebody else.'

'Yes, that, of course, but they wouldn't have done for me even if they had gone through with it. They were either the smart hardboiled type, always wisecracking and making one feel like a piece of cheese, or the intellectual kind that wanted to mould me. I couldn't keep up with them. We weren't batting in the same league. But Vee, she's different. I've never been a brainy

sort of guy, and what I want is a wife with about the
same amount of grey matter I have, and that's how Vee
stacks up. Do you remember Clarice Burbank?'

'Was she the Russian ballet one?'

'No, that was Marcia Ferris. Clarice was the one who
made me read Kafka. And the reason I bring her up is
that Vee would never dream of doing a thing like that.'

'She probably thinks Kafka's a brand of instant coffee
with ninety-seven per cent of the caffeine extracted.'

'Exactly. She's just a sweet simple English girl with
about as much brain as would make a jay bird fly
crooked, and that's the way I want her.'

'Well, that's fine.'

'You bet it's fine.'

'When is the wedding to be?'

Tipton looked cautiously over his shoulder, as if to
assure himself that they were alone and unobserved.

'Can you keep a secret?'

'No.'

'Well, try to keep this one, because if it gets out, all
hell will break loose. Before I left for America, Vee and I
fixed the whole thing up. We decided that a big Society
wedding was a lot of prune juice and we wanted no piece
of it. We're going to elope. I'm off to London tomorrow,
and a couple of days after that we'll be married at the
registrar's.'

'What!'

'Yes, sir, right plumb spang at the registrar's.'

'You mean that two days from now –'

'I'll be picking the rice out of my hair, if registrars
throw rice when they marry you.'

Sandy was breathing emotionally. How wrong, she
felt, how terribly misguided she had been in urging Sam
to accept the syndicate's offer, and how thankful she
was that it was not too late to tell him so.

'I think that's wonderful, Tippy,' she said, speaking
with some difficulty and raising her voice a little so as to

be audible over the soft music which was filling the room. 'I'm sure you're doing the right thing.'

'Me, too.'

'Who wants a lot of bishops and assistant clergy?'

'Just how I feel. Let the bishops bish elsewhere and take the assistant clergy with them.'

'I know you'll be happy.'

'I don't see how I can miss.'

'As happy as I'm going to be.'

'Don't tell me you're thinking of jumping off the dock, too?'

'One of these days. In your wanderings about Blandings Castle have you happened to meet a character called Whipple?'

'I've seen him around. Husky guy with a cauliflower ear. Is he the one?'

'He's the one.'

'He looks all right to me.'

'To me also. You don't know where he is, do you?'

'Sure. I heard Willie Allsop telling him old Emsworth wanted to see him down at the pig sty. You'll find him in the pig sty, you can tell him by his hat,' quoted Tipton blithely.

'Thanks, Tippy,' said Sandy, equally blithely. 'I'll be on my way.'

2

It is never easy for a young man to be carefree and at his ease when, after having had difficulties with the police, he finds himself immured by them in a smelly shed, and Sam, sitting on a broken wheelbarrow and breathing in the scent of manure and under-gardeners, did not come within measurable distance of achieving this frame of mind. He would have been only too happy to look on the bright side, if there had been a bright side, but as far as he could discern there was not. He viewed the future with the gravest misgivings.

He was not quite sure what was the penalty for the crimes he had committed, but he had an idea that it was something lingering with boiling oil in it, and the thought depressed him. He was also feeling puzzled. Not being a mind reader, he was unaware of Constable Evans's change of plan and he could not imagine why, having uttered those fateful words 'You're pinched', he had faded so abruptly from the scene.

Rightly concluding that speculation on this point was idle, he turned his mind to thoughts of Sandy, but these merely deepened his despondency. Gally, that blithe optimist, seemed to be under the impression that he had only to meet her and their relations would instantly revert to their original cordiality, but he could not bring himself to share this sunny outlook. To begin with, he had called her in his heat not only a ginger-haired little fathead but other things equally offensive to a girl of spirit. She could hardly be expected to forgive that without straining a sinew.

And secondly there was this matter of the prison term that overshadowed his future. In due course, he presumed, he would come up before some sort of tribunal and be sentenced to whatever it was you got for stealing watches and assaulting the police, and few girls care to marry a jailbird, with all the embarrassments such a union involves. It is never nice for a young bride to have to explain to hosts and hostesses that the reason her husband has not come to the party is that he has just started another stretch in Pentonville.

The poignancy of it all swept over him like a wave, and he heaved a sigh. At least, that was what he had intended to heave, but by some miscalculation it came out like the wail of a banshee, and from somewhere outside a startled voice cried 'Oo!', causing hope to stir in a heart that had practically forgotten what the word meant. The voice had sounded feminine, and women, he knew, can generally be relied upon to bring aid and comfort to those in trouble. Poets have stressed this. The lines 'When pain and anguish wring the brow, a ministering angel thou' floated into his mind. Scott had written that, and you could rely on a level-headed man like Scott to know what he was talking about. There was a small window in one wall of the shed, its glass long broken and the vacant space given over to spiders' webs. He approached it, and said:

'Is that somebody out there?' and simultaneously the voice said:

'Is that somebody in there?' and it was as if he had been seated in an electric chair at its most electric. What he could see of the outer world, which was not much, swam before his eyes. Even when merely saying 'Oo!' the voice had seemed familiar. Now that it had become more talkative, he had no difficulty in recognizing it.

'Is that you, Sandy?' he said, and then, speaking diffidently for he had no means of knowing how such a plea would be received by one in whose estimation he had fallen so extremely low, 'Would you mind letting me out?'

'Why don't you *come* out?'

'I can't. He's bolted the door.'

'Who has?'

'The cop. I'm under arrest.'

'Under what?'

'Arrest. A for apple, R for –'

'Oh, Sam, *darling*!'

Again Sam experienced that electric chair illusion. There was something sticking in his throat that seemed about the size of a regulation tennis ball. He swallowed it, and said in a hushed voice:

'Did you say darling?'

'You bet I said darling.'

'You mean – ?'

'Of course I do.'

'Everything's really all right?'

'Everything. Sweethearts still.'

Sam drew a deep breath.

'Thank God! I've been feeling suicidal.'

'Same here.'

'I wish I had a quid for every time I've thought of shoving my head in the gas oven.'

'Me, too.'

'I'm sorry I called you a ginger-haired little fathead, Sandy.'

'You were one hundred per cent right. I was a ginger-haired little fathead. Wanting you to take that syndicate offer. I must have been crazy.'

'You mean you've changed your mind?'

'I'll say I have. I've seen Tipton and he's going to elope with Veronica Wedge the day after tomorrow. He's practically married already. But we mustn't stand here talking. I'll let you out, and then you can tell me what on earth all this cop-arrest stuff is about.'

It took Sam only a few moments to do this after the door had opened, and Sandy listened with growing concern.

'Oh, Sam!' she wailed and flung herself into his arms as Gally had recommended, and Gally, coming up as she did so, surveyed them with fatherly approval.

'Satisfactory,' he said, 'but there's no time for that sort of thing now. You're on the run, my boy, so start running. Constable Evans should be with us at any moment, and you'll look silly if he finds you here. He will approach, I presume, when he does approach, via the kitchen garden, so make for the front entrance and work your way to the billiards room or the smoking-room or wherever else you see fit so long as it offers sanctuary. Sandy and I will wait here to receive him. You are possibly wondering,' he said after Sam, recognizing his advice as good, had taken it, 'how I happened to pop up out of a trap like this at the centre of things. Very simple. I was trying to find our young friend to tell him I thought you were favourably disposed to a reconciliation, and I looked in at Beach's pantry to ask if he had seen him. Constable Evans was there, speaking on the telephone, and Beach informed me in an undertone that the zealous officer had locked Sam in the shed by the pig sty and was calling up his reserves. One guesses what was in his mind. At their previous meeting Sam had – rightly or wrongly – plugged him in the eye and he shrank from having it happen again. No doubt it was his prudent intention, when his assistant arrived, to let him go in first and see what would develop. If eyes are to be plugged, your cautious constable always prefers them to be the other fellow's. And talking of eyes, I think it would be a graceful act and one which would help to make Sam's day if you were to dispense with those ghastly spectacles of yours.'

'Don't you like them?'

'No, I don't.'

'Nor does Sam. He said they made me look like a horror from outer space.'

'He flattered you. Take them off and jump on them.'

'Right,' said Sandy, and did so.

'And now,' said Gally, having viewed the remains with satisfaction, 'if you glance to your left, you will see Evans and friend heading our way, prowling and prowling like the troops of Midian in the well-known hymn. I think perhaps you had better let me do the talking. It was an axiom in the old Pelican days that in all matters involving the boys in blue it was wisest to leave the *pourparlers* to Galahad Threepwood. These conferences with the cops call for delicacy and tact. Good evening, officers. Welcome to Blandings Castle and all that sort of thing.'

The two constables made an intimidating pair. A pen

portrait of Officer Evans has already been given and it need only be said of Officer Morgan, his brother-in-arms, that he resembled him so closely as to create in the mind of anyone encountering them in each other's company the illusion that he was seeing double. Only the former's rich black eye served to distinguish him.

'Pleasant after the storm, is it not?' said Gally. 'So you're out for a country ramble? Taking it easy among the buttercups and daisies, eh? Having a good loaf, are you?'

Constable Evans, resentful of the implication that the police force of Market Blandings lived for pleasure alone, replied that this was far from being the case. He and his colleague, he said, had come to make an arrest, and Gally raised his eyebrows.

'Not my brother's pig, I trust?'

'No, sir,' said the constable shortly. 'Man wanted for theft from the person and obstructing the police in the execution of their duty.'

'Any clue as to his whereabouts?'

'He's in that shed.'

Gally adjusted his monocle and looked in the direction indicated. He was plainly puzzled.

'That shed?'

'Yes, sir.'

'The one over there?'

'Yes, sir.'

'The one with the tiled roof?'

'Yes, sir.'

Gally shook his head.

'I think you're mistaken, my dear fellow. This lady and I were peeping in there only a moment ago, and the place was empty. Well, when I say empty, we noticed an old wheelbarrow and two or three flower pots and, if I remember rightly, a dead rat, but certainly no fugitive from justice. What gives you the impression that he's there?'

'I locked him in myself.'

'In that shed?'

'Yes, sir.'

'Or are you thinking of some other shed?'

'No, sir, I am not thinking of some other shed.'

'Well, it's all very mysterious,' said Gally. An idea seemed to strike him. 'He wasn't a midget, was he?'

'No, sir.'

'I thought he might have been hiding behind one of the flower pots, which would have accounted for our not seeing him. Then I must confess myself baffled. How he managed to get out of that shed is beyond me. Door locked, no other exit. It's the sort of thing Houdini used to do. I wonder . . . no, that can't be right. I was thinking he might have been one of those Indian fakirs who dematerialize themselves and reassemble the parts elsewhere, but then he wouldn't have bothered to unlock the door, and it was open when we looked in. The whole thing's inexplicable. I doubt if we shall ever get to the bottom of it.'

A dark flush had appeared on Constable Evans's granite face. He was by no means an unintelligent man, and with a swiftness which Lady Hermione herself could not have exceeded he had reached the conclusion that Gally was responsible for the disappearance of his quarry. But he did not dare to put his conviction into words. Gally, whatever his moral defects, was an inmate in good standing of Blandings Castle, and a respect for Blandings Castle had been instilled into him from his Sunday School days. There was nothing to do but say 'Ho!', so he said it. Constable Morgan, a man of deep reserves, said nothing, and after a few more sympathetic comments on a mystery which in his opinion, he said, would rank for ever with those of the *Marie Celeste* and The Man In The Iron Mask, Gally resumed his progress to the house, apparently unaware of the long lingering looks which both officers of the law were directing at his retreating back.

'Too bad,' he said as he and Sandy went on their way. 'One's heart bleeds for Constable Evans and his strong silent friend whose name did not crop up in the course of our conversation. I can readily imagine what a disappointment this must have been to them. I have known a great many policemen in my time, and they all told me that nothing gave them that disagreeable feeling of flatness and frustration more surely than the discovery, when they went to make an arrest, that the fellow they were after wasn't there. It must be like opening your Christmas stocking as a child and finding nothing in it. Still, one must not forget that these setbacks are sent to us for our own good. They make us more spiritual. Tell me,' said Gally, abandoning a painful subject, 'about you and Sam. What I saw gave me the impression that your hearts were no longer sundered. Correct?'

'Quite correct.'

'Excellent. What was it the poet said about lovers' reconciliations?'

'I don't know.'

'Nor do I, but it was probably something pretty good. I suppose you're feeling happy?'

'Floating on air.'

'Great thing, young love.'

'Nothing to beat it. Were you ever in love, Gally?'

'Very seldom out of it.'

'I mean really in love. Didn't you ever want to marry someone who was the only thing that mattered to you in the whole world?'

Gally winced a little. She had reopened an old wound.

'Yes, once,' he said briefly. 'Nothing came of it.'

'What happened?'

'My old father didn't approve. She was what was

called a serio on the music halls. Sang songs at the
Oxford and the Tivoli. Dolly Henderson was her name.
He put his foot down. Painful scenes. Raised voices.
Tables banged with fists. Not sure a father's curse
wasn't mentioned. I was shipped off to South Africa, and
while I was there she married someone else. Chap
named Jack Cotterleigh in the Irish Guards.'

'Poor Gally!'

'Yes, I must say I didn't like it much. But it was a long
time ago, and nobody's going to ship Sam off to South
Africa. By the way, I take it that when you were fixing
things up with him, you waived your objections about
the syndicate?'

'You bet I did.'

'Sensible girl. You won't regret it.'

'I know I won't. Tipton's getting married the day after
tomorrow. At the registrar's.'

'You don't say? Is that official?'

'He told me himself. Dead secret, of course.'

'Naturally. Though I wish I could tell Clarence. It
would relieve his mind to know that the big wedding is
off.'

'Why?'

'No wedding, no speech and, above all, no top hat.
Clarence has always been allergic to top hats. Strange
how tastes differ. I like them myself, particularly when
grey. There were days in my youth when the mere sight
of a bookie whose account I had not settled would make
me shake like a leaf, but slap a grey top hat on my head
and I could face him without a tremor. And now, I
suppose,' said Gally, as they came into the house, 'you
will be wanting to go in search of Sam?'

'I thought I might.'

'Well, try to cheer him up. For some reason he has
seemed to me nervous and depressed since he got here.
As for me, I think I'll go and have a talk with Clarence. I
always find his society stimulating.'

3

Gally was humming the refrain of one of Dolly Henderson's songs as he made for Lord Emsworth's study. Odd, he was thinking, how after thirty years he could still have that choked-up feeling when he thought of her. Oh well, what had happened had probably been all for the best. Pretty rough it would have been for a nice girl like Dolly to be tied up with a chap like him, he felt, for he had never had any illusions about himself. His sisters Constance, Julia, Dora and Hermione had often spoken of him as a waster, and how right they were. His disposition was genial, he made friends easily and as far as he could recall had never let a pal down, but you couldn't claim that as a life partner he was everybody's cup of tea. And people who knew them had described Dolly and Jack as a happy and devoted couple, so what was there to get all wistful and dreary about?

Nevertheless, all this marrying and giving in marriage that was going on around one did rather encourage melancholy thoughts of what might have been. Tipton was marrying Veronica, Sam was marrying Sandy, Wilfred Allsop, so Tipton informed him, was marrying that large Simmons girl. Good Lord, he told himself with a sudden twinge of alarm, for all he knew Clarence might have relaxed his vigilance and be in danger of marrying Dame Daphne Winkworth. Once this sort of thing started, you never knew where it would stop.

And it was as this disquieting thought flitted through his mind that the door of the study opened and he saw Dame Daphne coming out of it. She disappeared along the corridor and the next moment he was bustling into the study, all brotherly concern.

'Ah, Galahad,' said Lord Emsworth, glancing up from his pig book, 'I was hoping you might look in. A most peculiar thing has happened.'

Gally was in no mood to hear whatever it was that had struck his brother as peculiar.

'Are you crazy, Clarence?' he said. 'Have you forgotten what I told you?'

'Yes,' said Lord Emsworth, who always did. 'What was it you told me, Galahad?'

'On no account to allow yourself to be alone with the female whom, but for the luck of the Emsworths, you might have married twenty years ago. Your old girl friend Dame Daphne Winkworth. How could you be so criminally rash as to hobnob with her?'

'But, my dear fellow, how could I help it? She came in. I could hardly forcibly eject her.'

'What were you talking about?'

'Oh, various things.'

'The dear old days?'

'Not to my recollection.'

'Then what?'

Lord Emsworth searched a treacherous memory. Recalling what anyone had talked about two minutes after the conclusion of the conversation was always a taxing task for him.

'Was any mention made of the *Indian Love Lyrics*?'

'I don't think so. She was speaking, now that I remember, of someone called . . . now what was he called? . . . yes, I have it, someone called Allsop. The name was strange to me. Have you ever heard of an Allsop?'

'You have a nephew of that name.'

'Are you sure?'

'If you don't believe me, look in Debrett. Wilfred Allsop. What was she saying about Wilfred?'

'As far as I could make out, she is not going to employ him as a music master at her school. She did not like him getting intoxicated.'

'Intoxicated?' Gally was surprised. 'Even at the old

Pelican it had been unusual for members to get into that
condition in the middle of the afternoon. He felt that
there must be more in his nephew Wilfred than he had
suspected. 'Blotto, do you mean? Pie-eyed?'

'So she said. It appears that her son . . . I forget his
name . . .'

'Huxley.'

'Of course yes, Huxley. It appears that Huxley was
passing along the passage leading to the Garden Suite
and Wilfred Allsop was standing there singing drunken
songs. And only yesterday the boy had found him
drinking heavily by the pig sty. He of course told his
mother, and she has cancelled Wilfred Allsop's
appointment. I am not sure that I altogether blame her.
She seemed to fear that I might be offended, but I quite
see her point of view. I have never been the headmistress
of a girls' school myself, but if I were, I should certainly
think twice before engaging an alcoholic music master.
Such a bad example for the pupils.'

'And that was all? She didn't go on to more tender and
sentimental subjects?'

'Not as far as I recall. We talked about pigs. She is
interested in pigs. I was surprised how interested she
seemed to be.'

Gally's monocle sprang from its place. He called
loudly on the name of his Maker.

'The thin end of the wedge! Clarence, you must get
this woman out of the house and speedily, or you
haven't a hope of avoiding matrimony. It's the case of
Puffy Benger all over again. The same insidious tactics.
With Puffy the girl started by talking to him about his
approach putts – he was a keen golfer – and little by
little and bit by bit she went on till she had him reading
Pale Hands I Loved Beside The Shalimar to her, and
that was the end. I tell you solemnly that unless you act
promptly and firmly and heave this woman out on the

seat of her pants while there is yet time, you're a dead snip for the wedding stakes. She's closing in on you, Clarence, closing in on you.'

'You appal me, Galahad!'

'That's what I'm trying to do. Well, there you are. You have been warned,' said Gally, and stumped out, feeling that he had done all that man could do to save a loved brother from the fate that is worse than death.

Closing the door, he remembered that at the start of their interview Clarence had said something that had aroused his curiosity, though at the time more urgent matters had prevented him giving his mind to it. Something about something being peculiar or something peculiar having happened or something. He opened the door and poked his head in.

'What was that you said just now?' he asked.

'Eh?' said Lord Emsworth, who appeared dazed.

'The peculiar thing?'

'Eh?'

'Pull yourself together, Clarence. You said a peculiar thing had happened.'

'Oh, that?' said Lord Emsworth, coming out of his trance. 'It was nothing really, but it struck me as odd. I was looking through my desk, trying to find the annual report of the Shropshire, Herefordshire and South Wales Pig Breeders' Association, which Miss Callender must have hidden away somewhere with her infernal tidying up, and I came on a manila envelope. I opened it, and inside it was another envelope addressed to Tipton Plimsoll. I couldn't imagine how it had come there. So I rang for Miss Callender and asked her to take it to Tipton. I hope the delay in delivering it will not have caused him any inconvenience.'

11

1

Sandy, meanwhile, though she would have preferred to stay talking to Sam in the billiards room in which he had taken refuge, had gone to her office in the small room off the library to resume her work. She was a conscientious secretary and had always felt that as she was paid a salary, she should try to earn it. It was this defect in her character that so exasperated Lord Emsworth. His ideal secretary would have been one who breakfasted in bed, dozed in an armchair through the morning, played golf in the afternoon and took the rest of the day off.

But though she had sat down at her desk full of zeal and though there was still plenty to be done in the way of cleaning the Augean stables of her employer's correspondence, she found a strange difficulty in concentrating on the task in hand. And she had fallen into a trance as deep as any of Lord Emsworth's, when the bursting open of the door brought her back to the present, and after blinking once or twice she was able to identify her visitor as Gally. It seemed to her that he was agitated about something, and her diagnosis was perfectly correct. It was not easy to make Gally lose his poise. Throughout his long life a great number of people ranging from schoolmasters and Oxford dons to three-card trick men on race trains had attempted the feat, but always without success. It had been left for his brother Clarence to succeed where so many had failed. He spoke without wasting time on preliminaries.

'That letter? Have you got it?'

'What letter? I've got about a hundred, and all of them ought to have been answered weeks ago.'

'The Tipton letter Clarence gave you.'

'Oh, that one? No, I haven't got it. I gave it to Beach to give to him.'

'Death, damnation and despair!' said Gally.

He bounded from the room as rapidly as he had bounded into it. Mystified, Sandy returned to her work and was reading a communication from Grant and Purvis of Wolverhampton, who sold garden supplies and were at a loss to understand why they had received no answer from Lord Emsworth to theirs of the eleventh ult, when he reappeared.

'I thought Beach might still have it,' he said, 'but he hasn't. He gave it to Tipton a quarter of an hour ago. Curses on his impetuosity. May his next bottle of port be corked.'

No secretary, however conscientious, could have kept her mind on her work with this sort of thing going on. Sandy abandoned Grant and Purvis of Wolverhampton and their petty troubles.

'For heaven's sake, Gally,' she said, 'what's the matter? What's all this about Tipton's letter? What's wrong with him getting his mail?'

Gally, as a raconteur, had a tendency at times to elaborate his stories in a manner that tried the patience of his audience, but in his reply to her query he was admirably succinct, confining himself to the bare facts, and as these facts emerged the colour faded from Sandy's face and she stared at him with horror in her eyes.

'Oh, Gally!' she said.

He nodded a sombre nod.

'You may well say "Oh, Gally!" I wouldn't have blamed you if you'd said "Oh, hell!" The whole infernal mess is my fault. It shows what comes of trying to be clever. I thought it was such a bright idea to slip that letter in among Clarence's papers. The odds against him ever looking through them were at least a hundred to one, but, as so often happens, the good thing came unstuck. However, all is not yet lost.'

Sandy stared.

'How can you say that? What can you possibly do?'

'I can get hold of Tipton and tell him the tale and convince him that there is nothing in that letter to cause him concern.'

'If you can do that, you're a genius.'

'Well, we know that already. I'll go and find him now.'

The proposed search, however, proved unnecessary. Scarcely had he reached the door when it flew open and the object of it appeared in person.

'Ah, Tipton,' he said. 'Come on in. We were just talking about you.'

Tipton's demeanour had undergone a great change since Sandy had last seen him. Then the dullest eye would have recognized him as a young man sitting on top of the world. Now it was equally apparent that he had fallen off and come down with a bump. His brow was furrowed, his eyes dull, his mouth drooping. He was looking, in short, just as Sandy had seen him look when he had come to her for sympathy after being reduced to the status of a dear friend by Doris Jimpson, Angela Thurloe, Vanessa Wainwright, Barbara Bessemer, Clarice Burbank and Marcia Ferris.

'Oh, hello, Mr Threepwood,' he said, evincing no joy at seeing him. 'I didn't know you were here.'

'I am,' Gally assured him, 'and I may tell you I know all about that letter you have in your hand. Sandy and I were discussing it before you came in.'

'You were? Who told you about it?'

'Oh, various people. I have my spies everywhere. May I look at it?' said Gally, twitching it from his grasp without going through the formality of waiting for permission. He skimmed it in silence, his brows knitted, and when he came to the end gave a short, contemptuous laugh.

'As I expected,' he said. 'An obvious fake.'

Tipton's mouth, which emotion had caused to fall open like that of a mail box, opened an inch or two further. Gally's conversation often had this effect on people.

'You mean it's a forgery?' he asked with a sudden gleam of hope. This was something he had not thought of.

Gally shook his head.

'Not exactly that. The hand is the hand of Veronica, but the voice is the voice of her blasted mother.'

'You mean she made Vee write it?'

'Of course she did. It sticks out a mile. She probably stood over the poor girl with a horsewhip. Hermione dictated every word of this letter. Sift the evidence. On the second page the phrase "incompatibility of temperament" occurs. Do you suppose that that half-witted girl . . . pardon the word half-witted . . .'

'Don't apologize,' said Sandy. 'Tipton likes her that way.'

'So do I. So do we all. It's part of her charm. It's what endears her to everyone. If a girl as beautiful as she is had any brains, the mixture would be too rich. Where was I?'

'You broke off on the word "half-witted".'

'Ah yes. What I was going to say was that it is unbelievable that Veronica not only knows what incompatibility of temperament means, but is able to spell it. I yield to no one in my appreciation of her many excellent qualities, but her best friend would have to admit that she is about as dumb a brick as ever had a wind-swept hair-do, completely baffled by anything over two syllables. Look, too, at that "distressed" on page one. Is it conceivable that she would have put two s's in it if she had not had a mother to guide her? And another thing. Mark how wobbly the writing is. She was finding it hard to bring herself to push the pen. See that blotch that looks as if a wet fly had walked across the paper? An obvious tear drop. She might allow herself to be coerced into taking dictation, but she was dashed if anyone was going to stop her weeping bitterly. What we have before us, in short, is a communiqué from a girl whose heart is breaking with every word she is forced to write, but one who all her life has done what Mother told her to. I have watched Veronica ripen from infancy to womanhood, and if there was a single moment during those years when Hermione allowed her to call her soul her own, it escaped my notice. Ignore this letter is my advice to you, Tipton, my boy. Wash it completely from your mind.'

He probably had more to say, for he was a man who always had more to say, but Tipton rose to a point of order.

'But it doesn't make sense.'

'What doesn't?'

'Her mother twisting Vee's arm and making her write the thing. She was tickled to death when we got engaged.'

'Ah, but that was before you started going about the place telling everyone you had lost all your money. Hermione heard it from my brother Clarence, and it radically altered her views on your suitability as a son-in-law. I have no doubt that Veronica loves you for yourself alone, but Hermione doesn't.'

Tipton had begun to bloom like a flower beneath the rays of the sun, or perhaps it would be better to say like a string bean under those conditions.

'Then you think – ?'

' – That Veronica's sentiments towards you have not changed? I'm sure of it. I am vastly mistaken if you are not still the cream in her coffee and the salt in her stew, as the song says. Five will get you ten if you care to bet against it. Go and get her on the phone now and coo to her, and see if she doesn't coo right back at you. And when the voice off stage asks you if you want another three minutes, take them and blow the expense. There's a telephone in the library,' he would have added, but Tipton had already flashed from the room.

Sandy closed the door behind him. She looked at Gally with awe.

'So now I know what telling the tale means!'

'A very minor effort,' said Gally modestly. 'You should have caught me in my prime. One loses something of one's magic over the years. Still I think I accomplished my objective, don't you?'

'As far as Tippy is concerned, yes. But what happens when he gets her on the phone and she says she doesn't love him?'

'She won't. I cannot picture any niece of mine not loving someone as rich as he is.'

'You don't think it's only his money that's the attraction, do you?'

'Certainly not. They're soul mates. She has about as much brain as a retarded billiards ball, and he approximately the same. It's the ideal union and I am gratified that I have been able to do my little bit to push it along. Curious what a glow it gives one to see the young folk getting together. Which reminds me. I want to see Tipton about Wilfred Allsop.'

'What about him?'

'He's lost his job, and I am hoping to persuade Tipton to find him another.'

'You'll persuade him.'

'You think so?'

'Not a chance of him resisting when you start to tell the tale. You ought to have been a confidence man, Gally.'

'So others have told me,' said Gally complacently. 'I have always had that ability to touch the human heart strings. Why, in my early days, when I was at the top of my form, I have sometimes made bookies cry.'

2

The library was empty when he reached it, and he presumed that Tipton, having concluded a satisfactory talk with Veronica, had decided to join her in London without delay and had gone to the garage to get his car. The place to catch him would be on the drive outside the front door, and he made his way thither.

It was now getting on for the hour of the evening cocktail and a man less dedicated than Gally to the service of his fellows might have given up the idea of interviewing Tipton on Wilfred Allsop's behalf and hurried indoors. But where it was a matter of doing someone a good turn he was always willing to face privations. He hoped, however, that Tipton would not keep him lingering here too long, for already he was conscious of a dryness of the thorax which only a prompt Martini could correct, and at this moment, as if having divined his thoughts by extra-sensory perception, the man he wanted came bowling up in his Rolls Royce.

A glance at him was enough to tell Gally that his recent telephone conversation with Veronica Wedge must have taken place in what reporters of conferences between foreign ministers describe as an atmosphere of the utmost cordiality for his grin was the grin of a young man without a care in the world and he alighted from the car with a lissom leap that told its own story.

'Hello, Mr Threepwood,' he carolled. 'I'm just off to London.'

'To see the little woman?'

'That's right.'

'I take it, then, that the two bob or whatever it was

that you spent on that telephone call was not wasted. You found Veronica in genial mood?'

'You betcher.'

'And the wedding will proceed as planned?'

'Curtain goes up the day after tomorrow. Apparently you have to let these registrar birds have a day's notice.'

'That's to give them time to get over the shock of meeting the bridegroom.'

'I suppose they get all sorts?'

'Yes, it must be a wearing life. How about your witness?'

'That's all laid on. I'm taking Willie Allsop with me. He's up in his room, packing.'

'Ah? Well, before he arrives I should like to talk to you about Wilfred. Are you aware that he has lost his job?'

'I hadn't a notion. You mean the Winkworth woman isn't going to hire him as a music teacher?'

'No, she has cancelled the appointment and he is at liberty. It appears that she was tipped off that he had been singing drunken songs in the corridor.'

A grave look came into Tipton's beaming face. He shook his head.

'She wouldn't like that.'

'She didn't!'

'She's strongly opposed to anyone hoisting a few.'

'We all have our faults.'

'So what's Willie going to do?'

'Precisely what I wanted to see you about. I was thinking that you might come to the rescue and find him something.'

'Who, me?'

'You control a number of lucrative businesses, do you not?'

'Yes, I guess I do.'

'Such as – ?'

'Well, there's Tipton's Stores.'

'What could he do there?'

'Only go around in white overalls telling customers where to find the cleansers and detergents.'

'You can't think of anything better?'

'There's the ranch Uncle Chet left me out in Arizona. But can you see Willie as a cowboy?'

'Not vividly. But didn't your Uncle Chet own a music publishing concern in London? I seem to remember him saying something to me about it.'

'Good Lord, I'd quite forgotten. Sure he did. Aunt Betsy used to write songs, and the only way he could get them published was to buy out the publishers. It cost him a couple of million, but he said it was worth it just to keep harmony in the home. It's a very good firm, and I believe he'd got most of his money back when he passed on.'

'Then that's where Wilfred finds his niche. Unless you have any objections?'

'No kick from me. A guy who can play the piano like Willie can't go wrong in a music business. I'll see to it directly I hit London.'

'Excellent. Be large-minded when you're fixing his salary. Don't forget he wants to get married. And an idea strikes me. You're taking Wilfred to London. Why not take Miss Simmons, too, and make it a double wedding?'

The suggestion plainly appealed to Tipton. It was, he agreed, a thought.

'But what will Lord Emsworth say when he finds she's stood him up?'

' "Bless my soul!" no doubt, or something like that. No need to worry about Clarence. These shocks are good for him. They keep him alert and on his toes. It's something to do with the stimulation of the adrenal glands. And have no anxiety about the Empress's well-being. She'll be all right. Beach will give her her calories. He's done it before and can carry on perfectly well till Clarence signs up a professional. Go and sound out La Simmons and see how she feels about it. You'll probably find her with Wilfred.'

Tipton was convinced. He bounded off and in an incredibly short space of time was back with the news that all was well.

'I sold her the idea in sixty seconds flat. She's gone off to pack a suitcase.'

'Splendid. Then as I am becoming more and more conscious of the parched feeling that steals over one at this time in the evening, I will leave you. With, may I say, my best wishes and heartiest congratulations and all that sort of apple sauce. An uncle by marriage's blessing on you, Tipton, if you care to have it.'

3

As Gally made his way to the drawing-room, where the cocktails were, he was feeling that mellow glow which comes to men of good will when they have done the square thing by their fellows. It was always his policy, if he could manage it, to strew a little happiness as he went by, and there could be no gainsaying that in the last half-hour or so he had strewn it with a lavish hand. There were those of his acquaintance who had sometimes spoken with bitterness of his habit of playing the guardian angel – or, as they were more inclined to put it, of making a pest of himself by meddling in other people's affairs, but in this case he felt that he had meddled to good purpose.

As a rule his evening cocktail was a thing Gally liked to linger over, but this was only when he was in congenial company. Today he found himself alone. The drawing-room was empty when he entered it, and after a quick one of a purely medicinal nature he trotted off to enjoy another talk with Sandy Callender. She would, he knew, be interested to hear how his interview with Tipton had come out.

'Well, young Sandy,' he said, bustling into her office, 'your faith in me was justified. Tipton, as you anticipated, was as corn before my sickle. I played on him as on a stringed instrument. He's giving Wilfred a good job and Wilfred and the Simmons are going to London with him to make a double wedding of it. A nice smooth bit of work, if you ask me. And what have you been doing in my absence? Sweating away and earning your weekly envelope, I trust?'

'No, I had a slack period.'

'Sitting and thinking of Sam, no doubt?'

'As a matter of fact, I was listening to the six o'clock news on the radio.'

'Anything of interest?'

'Not much. Austin Phelps has got married.'

'I hope he'll be very very happy. Who the hell is Austin Phelps?'

'The tennis player, my good child. You must have heard of Austin Phelps. The Davis Cup man.'

'Oh, that chap? Yes, I've heard of him. Goes around shouting "Forty love" and "Love fifteen" and all that sort of thing. Phelps?' said Gally, his brow wrinkling. 'Austin Phelps? There's something about him I'm trying to remember, something apart from tennis. Somebody was mentioning him to me only a day or two ago in some connection. Was he divorced recently? Did he plunge into the Thames to save a drowning child? Or win a by-election in the Conservative interest? Or get arrested for drunk driving? Maddening how these things slip from one's mind. Phelps? Phelps? Austin Phelps? Ah, perhaps you can tell me, Sam.'

On Sam's face, as he came into the room, there had been the purposeful look of a man about to converse with the girl he loves. It faded as he saw Gally. He was very fond of that deplorable character, but there are times when the best of friends are superfluous.

'Tell you what?'

'All you know about a man called Austin Phelps.'

'He plays tennis.'

'I am aware of that. But what is there about him that gives me the idea that he is somehow significant? Has he a sideline of any sort?'

'I don't believe so. Just keeps on playing tennis as far as I . . . Oh, I know what's in your mind. The Drones Club sweep. Don't you remember I told you he was the second favourite? Tipton Plimsoll and he were running neck and neck for a while, but he had some trouble with his girl and the engagement was broken off. Luckily for me.'

'Good God!' said Gally, his monocle parting from its moorings, and simultaneously there proceeded from Sandy a cry or scream or wail similar in tone and volume to that of a stepped-on cat, and Sam soared some six inches in the direction of the ceiling. That cry or scream or wail or whatever it was had affected him much as if some playful hand had given him a hot-foot. Returning to terra firma, he touched the top of his head to make sure it was still there and stood gaping.

'W–?' he said. He had intended to say, 'What's the matter?' but the sentence refused to shape itself.

Gally looked at Sandy. Sandy looked at Gally.

'Shall I tell him, or will you?'

'I'll tell him,' said Sandy. 'I'm afraid you're going to get a shock, darling.'

Sam braced himself to receive it. He had been at Blandings Castle only a short while, but it had been long enough to enable him to know that anyone enjoying its hospitality must expect to get shocks. A few possibilities flitted through his mind. The house was on fire? Empress of Blandings had taken to the bottle again? Augustus Whipple was a pleasant visitor? Constable Evans had arrived with a search warrant? There was a wide area of speculation, and he was prepared for bad news in any form.

In any form, that is to say, except the one in which it came.

'Austin Phelps is married,' said Sandy, and it was as though he had been playing for the Possibles in that England trial game and one of the Probables had hurled himself on some particularly tender portion of his anatomy. He tottered and might have fallen had he not clutched at Gally, who said 'Ouch!' and disengaged himself.

'It can't be helped,' said Sandy. 'It's just one of those things. You mustn't take it too hard, angel.'

Sam, as he looked at her, felt his heart swell. He was conscious of a sudden increase of a love which had always been substantial. What a helpmeet, he was saying to himself, what a life partner. Not a word of reproach had she said for his folly in refusing the syndicate's offer. Was there another woman in the world's history who would not have touched on that at least briefly? Would Helen of Troy in similar circumstances have been able to restrain herself? Would Cleopatra? Would Queen Victoria? He very much doubted it, and advancing on her he took her in his arms and kissed her reverently. It was some time before either of them became aware that Gally was speaking.

'I'm sorry,' said Sam, feeling that an apology was due. 'I missed that. You were saying – ?'

Gally, momentarily shaken out of his customary calm, was himself again. His monocle was back in its place, and he was once more the Galahad Threepwood whom years of membership in the old Pelican Club had trained to resilience.

'I was expressing my contrition for having allowed this wallop to ruffle me,' he said. '"Twas but a passing weakness. I can now think clearly again. Obviously there is only one thing to be done. Our course is plain. We approach Clarence. How much money were you telling me you had managed to save? Two hundred pounds, was it not? And you require seven. Right. Clarence shall make up the deficit.'

If somebody had told Sam that he was looking like a startled sheep, he would probably have been offended. Nevertheless, that was how he was looking, for he was wondering if he could have heard aright. He had still to learn – what the female members of this man's family had discovered in their nursery days – that there were few things of which Galahad Threepwood was not capable.

'You're going to try to touch Lord Emsworth?' he gasped.

Gally frowned.

'I dislike that word "try". It suggests a lack of confidence in my powers.'

'But you can't ask him to lend a stranger like me five hundred pounds!'

'You are perfectly right. I shall make it a thousand. You will need a margin. One always does when one is doing up a house. No sense in trying to run the thing on too slender a budget. And don't forget that you are not a stranger. You are the author of the book which has been his constant companion for years. He loves you like a son.'

Sam remained unconvinced. He had always had a sturdy distaste for being a borrower.

'I don't like the idea of cadging money from Lord Emsworth.'

'I'll do the cadging. No need for you to appear in the negotiations at all.'

'I still don't like it. Do you, Sandy?'

'Yes,' said Sandy simply.

'Of course she does,' said Gally. 'She's got sense. She knows that when you want a thousand quid, you can't be finicky, you have to go to the man who's got a thousand quid, no matter what your scruples. And, dash it, my dear fellow, it isn't as if we are asking Clarence to make you a birthday present of this paltry little sum. You'll be able to pay him back when you sell the house. But I think I know what's really bothering you. You're thinking that being the author of *Put Me Among The Pigs* isn't quite enough to sway him, that something else is needed to give him that extra push which will send him racing for his fountain pen and cheque book, and possibly you're right. Anyway, it's best to be on the safe side. See you later,' said Gally, and with the impulsiveness which was so characteristic of him he dashed briskly from the room.

It was some moments before Sam spoke. When he did, it was in a low, rather trembling voice that showed that life in Blandings Castle had begun to take its toll of him.

'Sandy!'

'Right here, my king.'

'Have you known Gally long?'

'Quite a time.'

'Has he always been as jumpy as this?'

'More or less.'

'Where do you think he's gone?'

'Who can say? I should imagine he had a sudden inspiration of some kind. His sudden inspirations always make him quick on his feet.'

'Well, I wish they wouldn't. He made me bite my tongue.'

'Of course, there's another angle.'

'What's that?'

'He may just have thought we would like to be alone together for a while.'

'And how right he was,' said Sam, instantly forgetting his troubles and problems.

It was a quarter of an hour before Gally returned. There was always something about him that reminded those with whom he mixed of a wire-haired terrier. He was looking now like a wire-haired terrier which after days of fruitless searching for a buried bone has at last managed to locate it. He had the same air of quiet triumph.

'Sorry to keep you waiting,' he said.

'Quite all right,' said Sandy. 'We found lots to do.'

'You billed?'

'And cooed. Shall I tell you something, Gally? Sam's a lamb.'

'I dare say, but we need not dwell on that now. What concerns us at the moment is the lurking-in-sheds side of him.'

Sam winced.

'I would rather you didn't mention that word "shed" in my presence,' he said. 'It does something to me.'

'And how do sheds enter into it?' said Sandy. 'What, if anything, are you talking about?'

'I'll tell you. You are probably wondering why I left you so abruptly. I went to find that blot on the body politic Huxley Winkworth.'

'What on earth for?'

'I found him in the morning-room. He was cataloguing his collection of lepidoptera, and we had a long talk.'

'About lepidoptera?'

'About letting the Empress out of her sty. You don't know it, but it is the young thug's dearest wish to do this and see what happens. Several times he has attempted it, but on each occasion he was foiled by the vigilance of Monica Simmons. Staunch and true, steadfast at her post, she was always there to baffle him.'

'Lucky she was. Lord Emsworth would have a stroke if the Empress got loose.'

'Exactly. It would shake him to his foundations. Well, as I say, I found the child busy among the beetles and I put it to him squarely. Now, I said, was his moment. Monica Simmons had gone to London, the angel with

the flaming sword was no longer on the spot and the
coast was clear. Grasp this opportunity, I said, for it may
never come again. I had little difficulty in selling him
the idea. Sandy will tell you that I am a man not
without a certain persuasive eloquence. To come to the
point, he thought well of the scheme and assured me
that he would attend to it directly he had completed his
cataloguing. He estimated that it would take him about
another twenty minutes. So there you are.'

He paused as if waiting for a round of applause, but
Sam showed no enthusiasm.

'You'll probably take a low view of my intelligence,'
he said, 'but how do you mean "there we are"?'

Gally stared at him incredulously.

'Don't tell me you haven't got it? I'll bet Sandy has.'

'Of course. Sam lurks in the shed, Huxley sneaks up
on his nefarious errand, Sam pops out and grabs him. He
takes him to Lord Emsworth and tells the tale and Lord
Emsworth is so grateful that he can deny him nothing.
Then you go to Lord Emsworth and ask him to lend his
benefactor a thousand pounds and he says "Capital,
capital, capital" and there's your happy ending. Right,
professor?'

'Right to the last drop. You'd better be getting along,
Sam, and taking up your station.'

Sam displayed even less enthusiasm than before.

'You want me to go and sit in that blasted shed?'

'You've grasped it.'

'There's a dead rat there.'

'It'll be company for you.'

'And what's more I'm not at all certain there aren't
live rats, too. When I was there before, I kept hearing a
very sinister rustling. I won't do it.'

'Of course you will, my pet,' said Sandy briskly.
'Think what it means to us.'

'Yes, I know, but –'

'Sam! Sammy! Samuel, darling!'

'It's all very well to say Sam, Sammy, Samuel darling –'

'For my sake! The woman you love!'

'Oh, all right.'

'That's my brave little man.'

'But I do it under protest,' said Sam with dignity.

'Odd,' said Gally, as the door closed, 'that a single visit should have left him so prejudiced against that shed. You wouldn't think to look at him that he was the neurotic type. But you often find these fellows with tough exteriors strangely sensitive. It was the same with Plug Basham that time Puffy Benger and I put the pig in his bedroom.'

'Why did you do that, if you don't mind me asking?'

'To cheer the poor chap up. For several days he had been brooding on something, I forget what, and Puffy and I talked it over and decided that something must be done to take him out of himself. He needs fresh interests, I said to Puffy. So we coated a pig liberally with phosphorus and left it at his bedside at about two in the morning. We then beat the gong. The results were excellent. It roused him from his despondency in a flash and gave him all the fresh interests he could do with. But the point I'm making is that it was years after that before he could see a pig without a shudder. He took the same jaundiced view of them that Sam has taken of potting sheds. And Plug was an even tougher specimen than Sam. Curious. Oh, hullo, Beach.'

The butler had loomed up in the doorway, a portentousness in his manner that showed that this was no idle social call.

'Were you looking for me?'

'No, sir. For Mr Whipple?'

'Why do you want Mr Whipple?'

'Constable Evans and Constable Morgan are anxious

to interview him, Mr Galahad. They are waiting in my pantry.'

It was a sensational announcement, and it caused Sandy, the weaker vessel, to give a gasp that reminded Gally of the death rattle of an expiring soda syphon. Gally himself, true to the traditions of the old Pelican Club, remained calm.

'You mean they're back?'

'Yes, sir.'

'You amaze me. I thought we'd seen the last of that comedy duo. What brought them?'

'I informed Constable Evans on the telephone that the person I allude to was in residence at the castle, Mr Galahad. You will recall that I expressed to you my belief that he was a criminal and an impostor.'

'I remember that you did gibber along the lines you have indicated, but I thought I had reasoned you out of that silly idea.'

'I have returned to it, sir.'

'Well, you're wrong, of course, and those constables are going to blush hotly when they realize what asses they've made of themselves, but if they want Whipple, they'll find him down at the lake. He went to have a swim before dinner.'

'Thank you, Mr Galahad. I will notify the officers.'

The door closed. Gally uttered an impatient snort.

'What a curse zeal is! It's what makes Clarence disapprove of you so much. Beach has been zealous since he was a young under-footman. Never lets well alone. There have been lots of complaints about it. Well, this means we'll have to cut the Sam–Huxley sequence.'

'I was thinking the same thing myself.'

'Not that it matters. I can bend Clarence to my will perfectly adequately without it.'

'And the lamb Sam? What do we do about him?'

'We get him away.'

'So I should think, with this troupe of bloodhounds after him.'

'There's nothing to keep him here now that you and he have ironed out your little difficulties. Go and pick him up at the shed and take him to the garage and let him select the best car he sees there and drive to London. And tell him that speed is of the essence.'

'So he's stealing cars now as well as bicycles?'

'Yes, he's getting into the swing of the thing capitally. What are you waiting for?'

'I'm not waiting. I'm just going.'

'Well, go. And I,' said Gally, 'will be off to see Clarence.'

12

1

With an interview of major importance before him, the prudent man does not act precipitately. Someone younger and less experienced might have hastened immediately to Lord Emsworth's study without pausing to prepare himself, but Gally knew that on these occasions a stimulus is required if one is to give of one's best. His first move, accordingly, after Sandy had left him, was to make for the drawing-room. The cocktails there would, he feared, by now be mostly ice water, but there was no time for the leisurely glass of port in Beach's pantry which he would have preferred, and he had always been a man who could rough it when he had to.

The Martini which he proceeded to pour proved an agreeable surprise. It did not bite like a serpent and sting like an adder, but it was not without a certain quiet authority, and he had taken it into his system and was feeling much invigorated, when the door opened and his sister Hermione appeared.

Anyone who had seen Lady Hermione as little as ten minutes ago would have been astounded by her demeanour as she entered the room, for ten minutes ago she had been in the poorest of shapes. The failure of her expedition to the Garden Suite had left her shaken, and running over the details of the disaster in her mind as she sat in her boudoir she was still quivering. She seemed to hear once again her nephew Wilfred's sudden outburst of song, and she shuddered as she recalled it. That horrible noise had set every nerve in her body a-tingle. It would be too much, perhaps, to say of a woman of her strong character that she had the heeby-jeebies, but she was certainly emotionally disturbed. A psychiatrist, seeing her, would have rubbed his hands gleefully, scenting lucrative business.

But now her agitation had subsided and she was calm again. Smug, too, thought Gally as he eyed her. Acquaintance with her from their nursery days had made him expert at analysing her various moods, and he did not like the current one at all. Her air seemed to him the air of a sister who had that extra ace up her sleeve which makes all the difference. Nevertheless, he greeted her with a cordial 'Hullo, there' and prepared himself for whatever might be going to befall by taking another Martini and water.

The action drew from her a sniff of disapproval.

'I thought I should find you near the cocktail shaker, Galahad.'

'You wanted to see me?'

'Yes, there are several things I have to say to you.'

'Always glad of a chat.'

'I doubt if you will like this one.'

'Have you come to tell me that Dame Daphne Winkworth has tied a can to Wilfred?'

'I beg your pardon?'

'She isn't taking him on as a music master.'

'Indeed? No, I had not heard. But it was not Wilfred that I wanted to talk about.'

'Then would you mind saying what you do want to talk about? I'm a busy man and I have a hundred appointments elsewhere. I can't give you more than five minutes.'

'Five minutes will be ample.'

Lady Hermione sat down, and the smugness of her manner became more pronounced. Gally, who had been trying to think who it was that she reminded him of, suddenly got it. The Fat Boy in Pickwick. She had only

to say 'I want to make your flesh creep', and the
resemblance would be complete.

'A few minutes ago Veronica rang me up on the
telephone.'

'Oh yes?'

'She was radiantly happy. She had just been having a
long talk with Tipton.'

'Oh, yes?'

'And to cut a long story short –'

'Always a good thing.'

' – He told her he had read that letter –'

'The one you dictated?'

' – And was sure she had not meant a word of it. And
of course she said she hadn't. They are getting married at
the registrar's the day after tomorrow. I very seldom
approve of these runaway weddings, but in this case I
think they are quite right. I'm afraid their decision
affects you a good deal.'

'You mean about Sam Bagshott?'

'Is that his horrible name? I had forgotten. Yes, about
Sam Bagshott.'

'What do you plan to do?'

'What do you expect me to do? I shall tell him to leave
the castle immediately, and then I shall go to Clarence
and explain what has happened.'

'I see.'

'Where is he?'

'In his study, I imagine.'

'Not Clarence. This man Bagshott.'

'Oh, Sam? He was in that little room off the library
just now. The one Sandy Callender works in.'

'Thank you. There is no need for you to come,
Galahad,' she said some moments later, pausing outside
the library door.

'You wouldn't care to have me as a bodyguard?'

'I don't understand you.'

'Sam, when stirred, is apt to plug people in the eye.'

'I don't think I am in any danger.'

'Have it your own way. But be on the alert. The thing to do is to watch his knees. They will tell you when he is setting himself for a swing. Keep your guard up and remember to roll with the punch.'

'Thank you. Good-bye, Galahad,' said Lady Hermione coldly.

She went in and Gally, closing the door behind her, turned the key in the lock and trotted briskly away. His schedule called for quick action. He was sorry to have had to inconvenience his sister, but it was imperative that she remain in storage until the conclusion of his business talk with his brother Clarence. And the inconvenience would after all be slight. There were comfortable chairs for her to relax in and several thousand good books to curl up with if she wanted something to help her pass the time. It was with no burden on his conscience, such as it was, that he set out for Lord Emsworth's study.

His route lay through the spacious hall where the 'No smoking' and 'Kindly keep in line' signs had been, and as he descended the stairs he was aware of a measured voice speaking from that direction. It seemed to be urging someone to come to the castle with all possible speed, and reaching the hall he saw Beach at the telephone. The conversation, whatever its import, had apparently concluded, for the butler, with a polished 'Thank you, sir. I will inform Dame Daphne,' was hanging up the receiver.

'What was all that about, Beach?' he asked.

'I was telephoning the doctor on behalf of Master Winkworth, Mr Galahad.'

'He's ill, is he? Nothing trivial, I hope?'

'He has sustained a wounded finger, sir. The Empress bit him.'

'What!'

'Yes, sir. I have no information as to how it occurred.'

'I can fill you in. His one aim in life is to let the Empress out of her sty, and he must have sneaked off to do it, little knowing that she had a bad hangover and was spoiling for a fight with someone. She went on a bender yesterday.'

'Indeed, Mr Galahad? I was not aware.'

'Yes, she mopped the stuff up like a vacuum cleaner and today is paying the price. One pictures the scene. Huxley steals up and no doubt chirrups. The Empress winces. He continues to chirrup. She approaches the gate, cursing under her breath. He puts his finger in to raise the latch, and she lets him have it. I don't blame her, do you?'

'No, sir.'

'You take the broadminded view? You feel, as I do, that he was asking for it and deserved everything that was coming to him? I thought you would. Best possible thing that could have happened, in my opinion. It will teach him a lesson. I shouldn't wonder if this didn't prove a turning point in his life, and if anybody's life needs all the turning points it can get, it's his. The occasion, as I see it, is one for sober rejoicing. But I mustn't stay here chatting with you, much as I enjoy it. I have a business appointment. You don't happen to know if the constables found Mr Whipple, do you?'

'No, sir. The officers have not yet returned.'

'Well, give them my love when they do. Charming chaps, charming chaps,' said Gally.

He resumed his progress to the study. Opening the door, he halted on the threshold, staring, a startled 'Lord love a duck!' on his lips.

2

The sight that met his monocle was one well calculated to cause alarm and concern. Something had plainly occurred to upset the even tenor of his elder brother's life. Roget, searching in his Thesaurus for adjectives to describe Lord Emsworth as he drooped bonelessly in his chair, would probably have settled for stunned, flustered, disturbed, unnerved and disconcerted. Gally, who had a feeling heart, was disconcerted himself as he saw him, though, looking on the bright side, as was his habit, he felt that whatever had happened must have done his adrenal glands a world of good.

'Strike me pink, Clarence,' he exclaimed, 'what's bitten you?'

Lord Emsworth, though stunned, flustered and disturbed, was able to see that he was under a misapprehension.

'It was not I who was bitten, Galahad, it was Daphne Winkworth's son, I keep forgetting his name.'

'Yes, so Beach was telling me. But I'm surprised that you're taking it so hard. I should have thought you'd feel it was just retribution and the wages of sin and all that.'

'Oh, I do. Yes, quite.'

'Then why are you looking like the wreck of the *Hesperus*?'

Gally's sympathetic attitude was helping Lord Emsworth to become calmer. A kindly brother in whom one can confide always works wonders on these occasions.

'Galahad,' he said, 'I have just been through a most painful experience.'

'Don't you mean Huxley has?'

'It has left me shaken. Have you ever been face to face in a small room with an angry woman?'

'Dozens of times in my younger days. One of them spiked me in the leg with a hatpin. Yours didn't do that to you, did she?'

'Eh? Oh, no.'

'Then you're that much ahead of the game. Who was your angry woman? It couldn't have been Hermione, for

I happen to know that she is occupied elsewhere, so I take it it was the divine Winkworth. Am I right?'

'Yes, she burst in on me with the news about her son's finger, and do you know what she said? You will scarcely credit this, but she said the Empress was a savage and dangerous animal and must be destroyed. The Empress!'

'Gadzooks! Didn't you explain to her that the poor soul had a morning head?'

'I was too flabbergasted. I stared at her for quite a while, unable to speak. Then I fear I was rather rude.'

'Excellent. What did you say?'

'I'm afraid I told her not to be a fool.'

'You couldn't have done better. And then?'

'A violent argument followed, in the course of which I became still ruder. In the end she said she would not stay another day in the castle and flounced off.'

'What-ed off? Oh, flounced? I see what you mean.'

'I think what caused her particular annoyance was that while we were talking I telephoned the vet to ask if there was any danger of infection to the Empress.'

'A very sensible precaution.'

'It appeared to infuriate her. We both became very heated. I ought to have shown more restraint. I shouldn't have offended Daphne.'

'Why not? It was the consummation devoutly to be wished. Dash it, Clarence, you were in deadly peril from this woman. Already she had told you she was interested in pigs, and from there to getting you to the altar rails would have been but a step. Your attitude seems to me to have been exactly right. If poor Puffy Benger had had your courage and resolution, he wouldn't today be the father of a son with adenoids and two daughters with braces on their teeth. You have removed the Winkworth from your life. The shadow has passed. You have won through to safety.'

'Bless my soul, I never thought of that.'

'If you feel like doing the dance of the seven veils all over the castle, I shall have no objection. But you still have a careworn look. Why is that?'

'I was thinking of Hermione.'

'What about Hermione?'

'She will have something to say, I fear.'

'Well, when she says it, show the same splendid firmness you did in dealing with Ma Winkworth. Who's Hermione? A woman you have frequently seen spanked by a Nanny with a hairbrush. If she starts getting tough, remind her of that and watch her wilt. A fig for Hermione, if I may use the expression. Her views on the matter in hand don't amount to a hill of beans.'

Lord Emsworth's mild eyes glowed.

'You're great comfort, Galahad.'

'I try to be, Clarence, I try to be.'

Lord Emsworth fell into a meditative silence, but Gally's assumption that he was thinking of his sister and inwardly rehearsing things to say to her – probably out of the side of his mouth – was incorrect. When he spoke, it was of the Empress.

'What I cannot understand, Galahad, is how that boy was allowed to approach the sty. Miss Simmons positively assured us that she would be on the alert to see that he didn't. If I remember, she said in so many words that she would rub his face in the mud if he attempted to come near the Empress.'

Gally saw that the time had arrived to tell all.

'I'm afraid I have some bad news for you, Clarence. Miss Simmons is no longer with us. She's gone to London to get married.'

'What!'

'Yes, she's marrying Wilfred Allsop. You're losing a pig girl but gaining a niece.'

Lord Emsworth's eyes, no longer mild, shot fire through his pince-nez.

'She had no right to do such a thing!'

'Well, you know, love conquers all, or so I read somewhere. I suppose she couldn't resist the urge.'

'But who will look after the Empress?'

He had brought the conversation round to the exact point which Gally desired.

'Why, who but Augustus Whipple?' he said. 'I'm sure he will be delighted to act as understudy till you can fill the part elsewhere.'

Lord Emsworth blessed his soul.

'But, Galahad, do you think he would?'

'Of course he will. There are no limits to what Gus Whipple will do to oblige people he's fond of, and I know he feels that you and he have started a beautiful friendship. He will have to return to London shortly, but while he's still here you can rely on him. A nice chap, don't you think?'

'Capital, capital. Quite. But why should he have to return to London?'

Gally glanced over his shoulder. The study door was closed. He could not be overheard.

'This is all very hush-hush, Clarence.'

'What is?'

'What I am about to tell you. Whipple has got to go to London to try to raise some money. I know you will let this go no farther, but the poor fellow's heavily in debt, and what makes it worse is that the debt is one of honour. He got into a poker game at the Athenaeum the other night, and you don't need me to tell you what that means at a place like the Athenaeum, where they play for high stakes. Many a bishop there has come away without his apron and gaiters after an all-night session. Whipple lost his shirt. He gave IOUs to half a dozen of the members, and if he welshes on them, they'll kick him out of the club without a pang of pity.'

Lord Emsworth's pince-nez were bobbing at the end of their string like adagio dancers.

'You shock me, Galahad! How much does he need?'

'A thousand pounds. What you would consider a mere trifle, but to him a colossal sum. Let us hope he will succeed in borrowing it somewhere.'

'But, Galahad! Why didn't he tell me?'

'Why you?' Gally paused, astounded by a bizarre thought that had come to him. He looked at Lord Emsworth incredulously. 'You don't mean you would lend him the money?'

'Of course I will. The man who wrote *On The Care Of The Pig*! I'll write a cheque immediately.'

Gally's face lit up. He rose from his chair, patted his brother twice on the shoulder and sat down again, plainly overcome.

'Well, that would certainly be the ideal way of putting everything right. It never occurred to me to think of you. But there's just one thing. You had better make the cheque payable to me. Whipple is a very proud man and though I know he's extremely fond of you, you are after all a comparative stranger to him. He might refuse to accept money from you, but if an old friend like me offered it to him, that would be different. You see what I mean?'

'Quite, quite. Very considerate of you to think of it. Now where is my cheque book? It should be somewhere, if Miss Callender hasn't hidden it with her infernal tidying – '

He broke off. Lady Hermione was entering the study.

3

Lady Hermione, like her brother Clarence, was looking stunned, flustered, disturbed, unnerved and disconcerted, so much so that Roget, had he been present, would have got the impression that these things run in families. Her face had taken on a purple tinge and her stocky body seemed to vibrate. Gally, who was given to homely similes, thought she was madder than a wet hen, and he was right. Only an exceptionally emotional hen when unusually moist could have exhibited an equal annoyance.

It was Lord Emsworth whom she had come to see, but it was to Gally that she first addressed herself.

'How dare you lock me in the library, Galahad?'

Gally started.

'Good heavens! Did I?'

'I might have been there still, if Beach had not heard me calling and let me out.'

'You're sure it wasn't Beach who locked you in? He has a very subtle sense of humour.'

'Quite sure. I happened to try the door just after you had left, and it wouldn't open.'

'Probably just sticking.'

'It was not.'

'Doors do.'

'This one didn't. It was locked.'

'Then,' said Gally, generously accepting the blame, 'I'm afraid it must have been me, but if I did it it was purely inadvertently. You know how you turn keys absent-mindedly. I'm terribly sorry.'

'Bah!' said Lady Hermione.

Lord Emsworth had been listening to these exchanges with growing impatience. Though there was no actual written rule to that effect, it was an understood thing that his study was a sanctuary into which the most thrustful sister must not penetrate. Sisters who wished to confer with him were supposed to do it in the library or the amber drawing-room or somewhere out in the grounds. It was the one flicker of spirit the downtrodden peer had ever been known to show. So now he intervened in the debate with something which if not truculence was very near it.

'Hermione!'

'Well?'

'I am having an important talk with Galahad.'

'And I am going to have an important talk with you. I have just seen Daphne. She is furious. She says you were very rude to her.'

Lord Emsworth was now definitely truculent. The mere mention of that name plumbed hidden depths in him and sent his blood pressure soaring into the higher brackets.

'She does, does she? What did she expect me to be, coming in –'

'Flouncing in,' said Gally.

'Yes, flouncing in and telling me I must have the Empress destroyed just because she bit that beastly little boy –'

'Who started it,' said Gally.

'Exactly. He was trying to let the Empress out of her sty, and goodness knows what might have happened if he had succeeded. The meadow is full of holes and ditches. She might have broken a leg.'

'Two legs,' said Gally.

'Yes, two legs. Apart from the nervous strain. The least thing upsets her and makes her refuse her food. It might have been days before she would have taken her proper meals, and if she does not consume daily nourishment amounting to fifty-seven hundred calories, these to consist of protein four pounds five ounces, carbohydrates twenty-five pounds –'

For an instant it might have seemed that the afternoon's thunderstorm had broken out again, but it was merely Lady Hermione banging the top of the desk. She had absent-mindedly, as Gally would have said, possessed herself of a heavy ruler, and she was using it with a lot of wrist work and follow through.

'Will you stop babbling about that insufferable pig of yours! I did not come here to talk about pigs. You must apologize to Daphne.'

Flame flashed from Lord Emsworth's pince-nez. Just

so had it done when he was dismissing George Cyril
Wellbeloved from his employment for the second time.

'I'm blowed if I apologize!'

'Well spoken, Clarence. The right spirit. It is men like
you who have made England what it is.'

It was not Lady Hermione who said this, it was Gally,
and she gave him a look which would have shrivelled
anyone but an ex-member of the old Pelican Club.

'I don't want your opinion, Galahad.'

'I can applaud, can't I?'

'No.'

'Well, I shall. As I did, I remember, when I saw you
being spanked by our mutual Nanny with a hairbrush.'

Lady Hermione winced, as if the old wound still
troubled her. She was silent for a moment, but it was
not in her redoubtable character to let ancient memories
silence her for long. With another look of a kind which
no sister should have directed at a brother she resumed
her observations.

'Daphne says that unless you apologize she will
leave.'

'She must suit herself about that.'

'If Daphne leaves, I leave. For the last time, will you
apologize to her and have that pig destroyed?'

'Of course I won't.'

'Then I shall take the first train to London tomorrow.'

'Voules can drive you in the car.'

'I do not wish to be driven in the car. I shall go by
train, and before I go I have something to say which may
interest you. Has Galahad told you of the amusing
practical joke he has been playing on you?'

'Eh? What? No.'

'You should have, Galahad. It spoils a joke to keep it
up too long. This man he has passed off on you as
Augustus Whipple is not Augustus Whipple at all.'

'What!'

'He is some loathsome friend of Galahad's whom he

has sneaked into the castle for some purpose of his own.'

'I can't believe it!'

'Perhaps you will when I tell you that almost immediately after he arrived Beach took a telephone call from the real Augustus Whipple, speaking from the Athenaeum Club in London. Good-bye, Clarence. I shall probably not be seeing you in the morning.'

The door closed behind her, and Lord Emsworth, after blinking some six times in rapid succession, said:

'Galahad –'

'Clarence,' said Gally, in his enthusiasm cutting him short, 'you were superb. A colossal feat. We tip our hats respectfully to the man who can look Dame Daphne Winkworth in the eye and make her wilt, but when immediately afterwards he crushes Hermione and sends her, too, flouncing off, words fail us and we can only bow before him in silence, recognizing him as a hero and a daredevil the like of whom one seldom sees. And you will reap your reward, Clarence. You have won for yourself a full, happy life alone with your pig, a life entirely free from sisters of every description. And you deserve every minute of it. But I interrupted you. You were going to say something, I think? Was it about that absurd charge of Hermione's?'

'Er – yes.'

'I thought so. You are wondering if there was any truth in it. My dear fellow, can you ask?'

'But how very odd that Beach should have spoken on the telephone to someone claiming to be Augustus Whipple.'

'Not really, when you come to think of it. I can explain that. I explained it to Hermione, but she wouldn't listen. You know how Visitors' Day always takes it out of Beach. Exhausting work showing people about the place. He was half asleep when he answered the phone. Got the name wrong. That sort of thing's always happening. There was a girl I knew in the old days who was madly in love with a man called Joe Brice. Telephone goes one morning, voice says, "Hullo, Mabel or Jane or Kate or whatever her name was, this is Joe Brice. Will you marry me?" Naturally she says he can bet his Old Etonian socks she will and she asks where they can meet. He mentions a bar in the Haymarket, and she goes there and a chap called Joe Price, whom she hardly knew, leaps at her and folds her in a close embrace, and when she hauls off and socks him on the side of the head with a crocodile bag apparently filled with samples of ore from a copper mine, he gets as sore as a gumboil and reproaches her bitterly. "You told me only an hour ago you would marry me," he says. Took her quite a while to straighten the thing out, I believe. Oh, hullo, Egbert. You back?'

The words were addressed to Colonel Egbert Wedge, who had come into the room at this moment looking travel-stained but less tired than might have been expected after his long journey from Worcestershire.

'Just got here,' he said. 'I caught an early train. I stopped off for a quick one at the Emsworth Arms. Oh, Gally, that letter I was telling you to expect. Did you get it?'

'I got it.'

'Good,' said Colonel Wedge, greatly relieved. He might have known, he felt, that he could rely on Gally. 'What's become of Hermione? Beach told me she was here.'

'She left a few minutes ago.'

'Then I'll catch her in our room. She's probably gone to dress. Oh, Clarence,' said Colonel Wedge, pausing at the door, 'this'll interest you. While I was having my quick one in the Emsworth Arms bar, a fellow came in whose face I thought I knew, and he turned out to be Whipple, the chap who wrote that book you're always reading.'

'What!'

'Yes. I asked him what he was doing in these parts, and he said you had invited him to the castle but couldn't have him at the moment as you were in bed with German measles, so as he wanted badly to have a look at the Empress he had put up at the Emsworth Arms. There must be some mistake somewhere, because you don't look as if you had German measles. You'd better give him a ring and find out what it's all about. Well, I think I'll be going along and having a bath. I'm caked with dust and cinders.'

Lord Emsworth spoke in a low, quivering voice.

'One moment, Egbert. You say you are personally acquainted with Mr Whipple?'

'I've met him two or three times at the Athenaeum. Old General Willoughby takes me to lunch there occasionally.'

'Thank you, Egbert.'

A long silence followed the Colonel's departure. Lord Emsworth broke it, and there was infinite reproach in his voice.

'Well, really, Galahad!'

It had often been said at the old Pelican Club that there was no situation, however sticky, which would not find Galahad Threepwood as calm and cool as a halibut on a fishmonger's slab, and he proved now that this was no idle tribute. Where a lesser man with an elder brother looking at him as Lord Emsworth was looking would have blushed and twiddled his fingers, he preserved his customary poise and prepared to tell the tale as he had seldom told it before.

'I know just how you're feeling, Clarence,' he said. 'You're as sore as a sunburned neck, and I don't blame you. I blame myself. I ought not to have been guilty of this innocent deception, but it was a military necessity. This chap – his name's Sam Bagshott and he's the son of the late Boko Bagshott, whom you probably don't remember though he was a bosom friend of mine – is in

love with young Sandy Callender and there had been a
rift within the lute and it was essential that he clock in
at the castle and heal it. This I am glad to say he has
now done thanks to you extending your hospitality. And
I wanted to tap you for that thousand quid because he
needs it in order to marry her. In fact, from start to
finish I acted from the best and soundest motives, but
don't think I don't see your point of view. You naturally
jib at the idea of parting with a thousand of the best and
brightest – though it would only be a loan and you'd get
it back with interest – to someone you hardly know.
And you are perfectly justified in taking this attitude.
Don't dream of parting. I was wrong to ask you. Keep the
money in the old oak chest. It's a pity, though, because
if you did feel like paying out, you would be sitting on
top of the world. You've got rid of the Winkworth,
you've got rid of Hermione, and this way you'd be
getting rid of Sandy, too. I beg your pardon, Clarence?
You spoke?'

Lord Emsworth had not spoken. What had proceeded
from his lips had been a strangled cry. His pince-nez
were gleaming with a strange light.

'Galahad!'

'Hullo?'

'Do you mean that if I lend this fellow Boko
Bagshott –'

'Sam Bagshott. Boko's the father.'

'Do you mean that if I lend this Sam Bagshott a
thousand pounds, he will take Miss Callender away
from here?'

'That's right. But, as you say, there's no earthly reason
why you should – except of course that if you don't
she'll be here as a fixture. No doubt you say to yourself
that you are quite competent to give her the sack, but
are you? I doubt it. She would cry buckets and your
gentle heart would be melted. And as you could hardly
expect a young girl to stay here unchaperoned, that

would mean begging Hermione to return, and one presumes that Hermione would bring the Winkworth with her and there you would be, back where you started.'

Lord Emsworth drew a deep breath.

'I will give you that cheque, Galahad. I will write it immediately.'

Gally was astounded.

'You will?'

'Quite.'

'Capital, capital, capital,' said Gally. 'Thank you, Clarence,' he added a few moments later as he took the oblong strip of paper with its invigorating signature.

He rose. He glanced at his watch. There would, he was glad to see, be just time before the dressing-for-dinner gong sounded for a quick visit to Beach's pantry. He looked forward to it with bright anticipation. Not only would there be port there but in all probability an added attraction in the person of Constable Evans, with whom it was always a privilege and a pleasure to exchange ideas.

The P G Wodehouse Society (UK)

The P G Wodehouse Society (UK) was formed in 1997 and exists to promote the enjoyment of the works of the greatest humorist of the twentieth century.

The Society publishes a quarterly magazine, *Wooster Sauce*, which features articles, reviews, archive material and current news. It also publishes an occasional newsletter in the *By The Way* series which relates a single matter of Wodehousean interest. Members are rewarded in their second and subsequent years by receiving a specially produced text of a Wodehouse magazine story which has never been collected into one of his books.

A variety of Society events are arranged for members including regular meetings at a London club, a golf day, a cricket match, a Society dinner, and walks round Bertie Wooster's London. Meetings are also arranged in other parts of the country.

Membership enquiries

Membership of the Society is available to applicants from all parts of the world. The cost of a year's membership in 1998 was £15. Enquiries and requests for an application form should be addressed in writing to the Membership Secretary, Helen Murphy, at 16 Herbert Street, Plaistow, London E13 8BE, or write to the Editor of *Wooster Sauce*, Tony Ring, at 34 Longfield Road, Great Missenden, Bucks HP16 0EG.

You can visit their website at:
http://www.eclipse.co.uk/wodehouse

refresh yourself at penguin.co.uk

Visit penguin.co.uk for exclusive information and interviews with
bestselling authors, fantastic give-aways and the
inside track on all our books, from the Penguin Classics
to the latest bestsellers.

BE FIRST

first chapters, first editions, first novels

EXCLUSIVES

author chats, video interviews, biographies, special
features

EVERYONE'S A WINNER

give-aways, competitions, quizzes, ecards

READERS GROUPS

exciting features to support existing groups and
create new ones

NEWS

author events, bestsellers, awards, what's new

EBOOKS

books that click – download an ePenguin today

BROWSE AND BUY

thousands of books to investigate – search, try
and buy the perfect gift online – or treat yourself!

ABOUT US

job vacancies, advice for writers and company
history

Get Closer To Penguin . . . www.penguin.co.uk